The Mystery of the Jade Tiger

Nancy approached the oak trees and heard the sound of young voices. She walked into the stand of trees and found Jimmy Thieu handing Amy Kirkland a brown paper bag.

"Amy," Nancy said to the girl, "please tell me what's going on. To begin with, what's in the bag?"

Amy looked as if she might answer, but Jimmy said something in Vietnamese, and she clutched the bag to her chest.

"I'll tell you what's in the bag, Miss Drew," said a strange voice behind Nancy.

Nancy turned to look at who was behind her, but she wasn't fast enough. A gloved hand clamped over her mouth, and another hand held a knife to her neck.

"Amy is holding the jade tiger," the voice continued. "And she's going to give it to me right now. Because if she doesn't, that'll be the end of Nancy Drew."

Nancy Drew
Mystery Stories

Available from MINSTREL Books

NANCY DREW MYSTERY STORIES®

104

NANCY DREW®

THE MYSTERY OF THE JADE TIGER

CAROLYN KEENE

A
MINSTREL®
BOOK

PUBLISHED BY POCKET BOOKS

New York   London   Toronto   Sydney   Tokyo   Singapore

This book is a work of fiction. Names, characters, places, and
incidents are either the product of the author's imagination or
are used fictitiously. Any resemblance to actual events or
locales or persons, living or dead, is entirely coincidental.

A MINSTREL PAPERBACK *ORIGINAL*

 A Minstrel Book published by
POCKET BOOKS, a division of Simon & Schuster Inc.
1230 Avenue of the Americas, New York, NY 10020

Copyright © 1991 by Simon & Schuster Inc.
Produced by Mega-Books of New York, Inc.

ISBN: 0-671-73050-9

First Minstrel Books printing December 1991

10 9 8 7 6 5 4

NANCY DREW, NANCY DREW MYSTERY STORIES,
A MINSTREL BOOK and colophon are registered trademarks
of Simon & Schuster Inc.

Cover art by Aleta Jenks

Printed in the U.S.A.

Contents

THE MYSTERY OF
THE JADE TIGER

1

A Friend in Need

"Isn't this the most perfect dress in the world?" Bess Marvin sighed and held up a short, ruffled pink dress with skinny shoulder straps. Straightening its hem, she carefully laid the dress on the Drews' living room couch. "It's a little tight," she explained, "but I'm going to lose five pounds before the wedding. What do you think? Isn't it adorable?"

Nancy Drew brushed back a strand of reddish blond hair and studied the dress. She bit back a smile. Bess was always going to lose five pounds. And she was always buying some adorable dress that didn't quite fit. Nancy tried to find a tactful answer. "Well," she said, "it's very pretty, but . . ." Nancy paused.

"But is it really the sort of thing you wear to be a bridesmaid?" asked Bess's cousin, George Fayne.

"Joanne says everyone should wear whatever they want," Bess said.

"That sounds like Joanne," Nancy said. Joanne Koslow, who was a few years older than Nancy and her friends, had been one of Bess's neighbors. Even as a little girl, Joanne had loved unusual clothing. She and Bess had been especially close friends. Now Joanne lived in northern California, where she worked as a photographer. She was marrying her boyfriend, Keith, and she had invited all three friends to the celebration. Nancy knew the wedding would be fun. She was also sure it would be anything but traditional. "Have you picked out your dress yet?" she asked George.

"No, she hasn't," Bess answered, looking genuinely worried. "And the wedding is less than two weeks away. George, we have to find you a dress."

Although they were first cousins, Bess and George were very different. Bess considered clothing to be one of the most important things in life. George, whose first love was sports, didn't care what she wore as long as it was comfortable. And their looks were as different as their personalities. George had an athletic physique, dark eyes, and short, curly brown hair. Bess's hair was long and blond. She had blue eyes and was shorter than her cousin.

Bess put her dress back in its box and tugged on her cousin's arm. "Let's go. I'm taking you shopping now."

"Help," George moaned.

Just then the door to Carson Drew's study opened, and Nancy's father stepped out, casting a worried glance at the cousins. "Is there a problem here?" he asked.

2

"Yes," George said quickly. "I'm being taken shopping against my will."

"I see," Mr. Drew said.

George shook off her cousin's arm and ran a hand through her short, dark hair. "Isn't there a law against that—forced shopping?"

Carson Drew, who was a well-known lawyer, tried to keep a straight face. "Not that I know of," he replied with a chuckle, "but I'll check into it. Speaking of things to check into, Nancy, do you remember Terry Kirkland?"

"You mean your friend in California?" Nancy asked. "The artist who makes those gorgeous stained-glass windows?"

"The very same. I just got a call from him. It seems he's having a rough time. His wife died a few years ago, and he's been raising his daughter, Amy, on his own. Well, his house was broken into twice in the last week. That frightened the sitter so badly she quit. Meanwhile, there's been a lot of interest in his work. He has a few big art shows coming up, but Amy's in school, so he can't take her with him. Naturally he's afraid to leave her alone."

"Can't he hire another person to take care of Amy?" George asked.

"I'm sure he could," Carson Drew replied. "But that isn't the sort of thing you do overnight. It's hard to find someone to trust with your only child. Nancy and I were unusually lucky to find Hannah."

Nancy's own mother had died when Nancy was very young. Even though she'd never met Amy, Nancy felt immediate sympathy for the girl. Nancy had been

3

raised by her father and their housekeeper, Hannah Gruen. To the Drews, Hannah was a great deal more than a housekeeper. She'd become part of their family, and Nancy couldn't imagine life without her.

Nancy's blue eyes, so much like her father's, sparkled as they met his. "Sounds as though Terry could use some help."

"I was thinking the same thing," Mr. Drew said.

George grinned. "I can see it now. Nancy could be a combination baby-sitter and detective."

"Exactly," Carson agreed. "What do you think, Nan?"

She didn't have to think about it at all. Although Nancy was only eighteen years old, she was an accomplished detective. She'd solved dozens of cases. The idea of helping Amy and figuring out who had been breaking into Terry Kirkland's house intrigued her. "Ask Terry when his next show is scheduled," she answered. "And tell him I'll be there."

"Ahem," Mr. Drew said. "I hope you'll forgive me, but I already took the liberty of doing that."

"And?" Nancy asked eagerly.

"He has three shows coming up next week," Carson replied. "They're all in northern California, so he'll only be gone a day or two at a time."

"That's the week before Joanne's wedding," Bess said. "She asked me if I wanted to fly out early. You know Joanne, she's doing everything herself and could use a few extra hands."

"I offered to help with the food," George said. "I figured I ought to put my catering experience to use." George had worked for a caterer when Nancy had

4

solved the mystery of *The Double Horror of Fenley Place.* "But then we found out that most of Joanne's family will be staying with her, and there really wasn't room for us."

"Terry's got a big, beautiful three-story house," Mr. Drew said thoughtfully. "Maybe what he really needs are *three* baby-sitter detectives."

Bess and George had often accompanied Nancy on her investigations. Bess wasn't quite as fearless as George, but their company always made solving mysteries more fun for Nancy.

"This is perfect!" Bess cried. "We'll go out early with Nancy. And while she works on the case, we'll work on the wedding."

"Actually, I think I'd rather work on the case," George said.

Nancy held up one hand, laughing. "Let's check with Terry first and make sure he's willing to take in all three of us. If he is, I'm sure we'll all find plenty to do."

Four days later, on a Friday afternoon, Nancy stepped out of the San Francisco airport terminal and into the warm California sunshine. "I can't believe this is winter," she said to Bess and George. "It must be over seventy degrees out."

"You're lucky. You've caught us during one of our February warm spells," Terry Kirkland said to the girls. He and his daughter, Amy, had met them at the gate. Terry was a tall, slim man in his late thirties. He had longish, slightly graying hair and a warm, easy-going manner that made Nancy like him at once. "I

5

hope you can get in a little sight-seeing while you're here," he said. "But if it's the city you want to see, I'm afraid it's going to be a drive. Cherry Creek, where we live, is a good hour and a half away."

That didn't bother Nancy at all. She had been in San Francisco before on other cases. This time she was looking forward to being in the country.

"Actually, it's perfect," Bess said. "You live about half an hour away from our friend Joanne."

"We really appreciate your letting us stay at your house," George said.

Terry grinned. "I think it will work out for everyone. I can't begin to tell you how glad I was when Carson called and told me he was sending the three of you."

"Me, too," Amy piped in. "Ever since our housekeeper quit, Dad's been worried about me."

Terry took his daughter's hand as they began walking through the parking lot. With her long, straight black hair, nine-year-old Amy resembled her Vietnamese mother.

"Lots of houses are broken into around here," Amy said matter-of-factly. "It's nothing to get scared about."

"As you can tell, Amy is the calm one in the family," Terry said as he opened the side door of his van. "So I'm panicking for both of us."

Terry loaded their suitcases into the back, and the three girls got into the backseat of the van. Amy insisted on sitting beside Nancy.

"How bad were the break-ins?" Nancy asked as Terry pulled out of the airport parking lot.

"In terms of what was taken, not bad at all," he answered. "The first time they took the stereo system and TV."

Nancy nodded. "Electronics are the easiest items to fence."

"I guess so," Terry agreed, "because the next time they came back and cleaned out my computer, the microwave, the answering machine, and Amy's portable cassette player. What's surprising is they didn't take any of the really valuable stuff—my glasswork."

"That would be much harder to resell," Nancy explained. "Someone might recognize your work. It sounds as if these were fairly typical robberies."

"Not exactly," Terry said. "After the first break-in I had a very sophisticated alarm system installed. Whoever broke in the second time dismantled the alarm as easily as unplugging a lamp."

"The thief must be a real pro," George observed.

The three girls caught their breath as Terry drove onto the Golden Gate Bridge. Below them San Francisco Bay sparkled in the late afternoon sunlight. Directly across the bridge lay the low green mountains and windswept coast of the Marin Headlands.

"We live over there," Amy said, pointing to the west. "Our house is all the way on the other side of Mount Tamalpais, beyond Stinson Beach."

Nancy glanced briefly at the beautiful coastline, but her mind was focused on the crime. "It sounds as if your thief was casing the house. The first time he, or she, broke in to see what you had that was worth stealing. Maybe there was only time to take the two

7

obvious things, the TV and the stereo. The second time was the real robbery."

"Or maybe it was two different thieves," George suggested.

"Good point," Nancy said.

"I just hope they got what they wanted," Terry said as he turned onto a winding mountain road. "All that matters to me is that they don't come back."

"Don't worry, Dad," Amy said confidently. "Nancy and I will get to the bottom of this."

Terry gave his daughter a wry smile. "I hope you work quickly."

Amy winked at Nancy. "No problem, Dad."

"I guess I've got a new partner," Nancy said, smiling at the girl. "I can always use another detective's help. There's only one condition. If things get dangerous, then you'll follow my instructions."

"Definitely!" Terry agreed.

Amy rolled her eyes at her father, then grinned at Nancy and said, "It's a deal."

More than an hour later Terry drove through the tiny town of Cherry Creek and into the steep green hills above it. The town itself was built along the Pacific Ocean. A row of shops led to a wide white beach edged with redwoods and scrub oak. Terry slowed the van as he turned off the paved road and onto a narrow dirt one, edged by a steep ravine.

"This is our driveway," Amy informed them. "You should see it when it rains—Mud Hill."

Nancy peered out the window curiously. There was no house in sight, just the rough dirt road, bordered by evergreens and eucalyptus trees. The van moved slowly up the hill.

"I'll probably be using the van while you're here," Terry said. "But you three can borrow my car. It's—"

His voice was cut off by a loud explosion. Amy cried out as the van swerved suddenly, teetered on the edge of the ravine, and then tilted to the left. Nancy braced herself against the seat in front of her as the van slid sideways down the ravine.

2

Three Strikes

The van slid to a shuddering halt at the bottom of the ravine. Nancy's side was pressed against the door. Amy was sliding toward her, and Bess and George toward Amy. Only the girls' seat belts kept them from crushing each other.

"Is anyone hurt?" Terry asked anxiously.

Nancy, Bess, and George assured him that they were fine.

"I'm fine, too," Amy said, obviously trying not to sound upset.

Terry undid his own seat belt and crawled out the passenger side of the van. Quickly he opened the side door and helped the girls out. Nancy pulled herself out of the van just in time to see a dark red sedan shoot past them and out the drive.

"Who was that?" Bess asked, her voice shaking.

Terry didn't answer. White-faced, he walked

around to the front of the van. Nancy heard him mutter an exclamation of disbelief. Following him, she saw that the van's front right tire had blown out.

"I don't understand it," Terry said. "I just put on new tires last month. I must have hit something that went right through the tire."

"What about the dark red car that just came out of your driveway?" Nancy asked.

Terry shook his head. "I've never seen it before."

"I didn't get a good look, but I think the driver was a large man with light hair," Nancy told him.

Terry thought a moment. "Well, I don't think it was anyone I know. It could have been someone who just turned onto the wrong driveway. Let's go up to the house. I'd better see about getting a tow truck and then call my insurance company."

Nancy, George, and Bess got their bags and followed Terry and Amy up to the house.

"What a place," Bess said as they reached the top of the drive and the Kirklands' house came into view. "It looks like a grown-up tree house!"

Built of wood and glass, its three levels spiraled into the branches of the surrounding redwoods.

"That was the idea," Terry explained. "As a kid, I was always crazy about tree houses. When it came time to build my own home, a tree house still seemed like a good idea. Fortunately, Lan, my wife, insisted I close it in with some walls."

He walked up to the side of the house, knelt down, and ran his hands along the earth. "We had another visitor," he said.

"How do you know?" Nancy asked.

11

Terry pointed to a spot that looked as if it had been dug up and covered over again. He picked up a rock, used it to dig down, and uncovered a severed cable. "This was my alarm system," he explained bitterly. "My *second* alarm system. I'd bet money that the phone lines have been cut as well."

"Why?" George asked, puzzled.

"When this alarm is set off or tampered with, it automatically sends a phone message to the police," Terry explained. "If the intruder knew enough to find underground cables, he probably knew about the phone connection, too." Terry sighed heavily and stood up, brushing the dirt off his hands. "Let's see what else our intruder was up to."

Cautiously they went inside. Nancy's first impression was that she was in the loveliest house she had ever seen. Terry's work was everywhere. All the windows were edged with delicate stained-glass designs. A pattern of green vines twined around the kitchen windows. Lilies framed the large window in the living room. There were lampshades and bowls, boxes and vases, all made of colored glass. It took Nancy a few moments to stop admiring the array of beautiful objects and realize that the house had been ransacked.

In the living room someone had taken a knife and ripped through the upholstered furniture. White stuffing poured out onto the rugs. Pictures had been pulled off the walls. The doors of an inlaid cabinet were flung open, its contents scattered all over the floor.

Terry stared at the chaos, looking stunned. "We

12

should make sure whoever was here is really gone," he said at last. "Amy, you stay down here."

Nancy volunteered to go with him, and together they checked the house.

"There's no one here but us," Nancy said when they had returned to the first floor. Amy ran up to her room when she heard it was safe to do so.

"What a mess!" Nancy exclaimed. "Do you know what was taken?"

Terry surveyed the damage and shrugged. "The place is such a shambles it's going to take a while to sort it all out." He picked up the telephone receiver. "Just as I thought," he reported, "the wire's been cut. I'm going to a neighbor's to call the police and the phone company."

He had just started out the door when there was a wail from upstairs. "Dad, come quick!" Terry turned at once and raced up the spiral staircase to the third floor. Nancy and her friends followed close behind.

Amy stood in the center of her room, tears streaming down her face. "They wrecked everything," she sobbed.

All the drawers had been pulled out of Amy's dresser. Clothing and toys were strewn about the room. An Oriental screen had been snapped in two, and the contents of Amy's desk drawers were dumped onto the floor.

"I know, honey. It's all right," Terry said, holding his daughter against his side. "We'll make sure they don't come back."

Amy wiped her eyes. "It's not all right," she said. "The thief took the trunk."

13

"Are you sure?" Terry asked in genuine surprise. "Why on earth would anyone steal that thing?"

Amy pointed to a space behind the broken screen. It was clear from the depression on the rug that there had once been a small trunk standing there.

"What was in the trunk?" Nancy asked Amy.

"It's where I kept my sweaters," the girl replied.

"Did you store anything else in there?" George asked. "Maybe you put something in there and forgot."

Amy shook her head. "Just sweaters."

Nancy's eyes scanned the room, finding no immediate clues. "What sort of trunk was it?" she wondered. "Maybe it's the trunk itself that's valuable."

"It isn't," Terry assured her. "It's just a cheap wooden trunk, but it does have a story behind it. Let me call the police, and then I'll fill you in."

A detective and a police lab technician arrived about an hour after the phone company's repair woman. Detective Brower, a large middle-aged man with thinning brown hair and a very red face, was in charge. He had the technician dust for prints, take fiber samples and photographs of the house, and make lists of everything that was stolen or vandalized. Terry had found that in addition to the trunk, a camera and a box filled with old silver dollars had been taken from his room.

"Was this camera valuable?" Detective Brower questioned.

"It was a good camera, but it really wasn't worth much," Terry replied.

"Did you have any film in it?" Nancy asked. "Maybe you took a photograph of something that someone didn't want you to see."

"Excuse me, miss," said Detective Brower in a sarcastic tone, "but who's conducting this investigation—you or me?"

"Detective Brower, allow me to introduce Nancy Drew," Terry said. "Nancy happens to be—"

"A friend of the family," Nancy broke in. She had a feeling that Terry was going to introduce her as a private detective. And she was almost certain that Detective Brower wasn't going to appreciate that.

"Fine," Brower said. "I'm glad you're friends, but I'll ask the questions here." He gave Terry a curious look. "*Was* there any film in the camera?"

"No," Terry said, not bothering to hide a smile. "And as for the coins, I took them to a collector a while back to have them appraised. She told me they were worth a few hundred dollars at most."

Brower shut his notebook with a snap and thanked Terry for his time.

"That's it?" Terry demanded. "This house has been broken into three times recently, and that's all you can say?"

The detective reached for his hat. "What do you want me to say, Mr. Kirkland?"

"You could tell me you're going to have the house watched," Terry said.

"We don't have enough people for that," Detective Brower said. He and the technician headed for the door. "We'll let you know what we find."

"I'm sure," Terry said, closing the door behind them.

Bess, who'd been watching the proceedings from a window seat, stood up indignantly and said, "I've certainly met more helpful police officers."

"I've met more helpful mosquitoes," Terry muttered.

"They were even worse the first two times," Amy said. "And they haven't told us anything. I bet Nancy and I will solve the case before they do."

Nancy was silent. She'd worked with police officers all over the country. Usually, they welcomed her help, but every so often she ran into someone like Detective Brower. She was going to have to be very careful around him.

"Why wasn't he more interested in the case?" she asked.

Terry shrugged. "The police department in this area is spread pretty thin. They have a lot of land to cover. Maybe Detective Brower has more important crimes to deal with. Maybe he's just been doing his job too long, and he's burned out."

"Or maybe he's just not very good at what he does," George suggested.

"It doesn't matter," Nancy said. "We'll just have to work around him. And speaking of work, we ought to start cleaning this place up."

Later that evening, after they'd eaten and Amy had gone to sleep, Terry and the three friends relaxed in the living room. Though the day had been hot, the night air was cool. Terry knelt beside the hearth and laid kindling for a fire.

Nancy watched him, her mind on the mystery. What was it the thief wanted? she wondered. The camera, the coins, or a trunk filled with a nine-year-old's sweaters? Or was it something else altogether?

"Terry," Nancy said, "in the first two break-ins the thief only took electronic equipment?"

"That's right."

"What if the thief wasn't interested in electronics at all?"

"Then why would he take them?" Bess asked.

"As a cover," Nancy answered. "Everyone expects that sort of thing to be stolen. What if whoever broke in was actually looking for something else, the coins or the camera or the trunk?"

Terry shook his head. "My stereo system alone was worth more than any of those items. Why would someone take all the valuable stuff first and then come back for the things that weren't worth anything?"

Nancy frowned, trying to fit the pieces of the puzzle together. "I'm not sure," she admitted. "Unless there was more than one intruder. Or unless what was stolen today was more valuable than you thought. You said there was a story behind the trunk?"

"The trunk came back from Vietnam with me," Terry began. "I was over there during the war as a soldier. I was very young and scared out of my mind. About six months into my tour our group teamed up with another unit.

"Anyway, I became friends with a guy from that unit named Nick Finney. We had the same birthday, and we'd both just gotten letters from our girlfriends in the States, telling us they had found new boyfriends.

"I only knew Nick for a couple of months before his unit was sent on one of those top-secret missions that

17

no one finds out about until an hour before you go. But Nick came to me right before they left and gave me that little wooden trunk. He asked me to hold on to it for him."

"What did the trunk look like?" George asked.

"It was about three feet by two, made of wood with brass bands around it and brass latches that were shaped like dragons. It wasn't worth more than thirty dollars, then or now, but Amy liked it. I think she associates anything from Vietnam with memories of her mother."

Nancy stretched out on the rug in front of the fire. "Nick never asked for it back?"

"He went on that mission and never returned," Terry explained. "He was declared MIA—missing in action. When I got back to the States, I looked up his family to give them the trunk. The problem was, Nick didn't have any family. He had been raised by a grandfather who died when he was in 'Nam. So I kept the trunk, sort of hoping that one day Nick would come back for it."

"Was there anything in it?" Nancy asked.

"I'll show you." Terry reached into a drawer in the cabinet behind him and pulled out a large brown envelope. He emptied its contents onto the rug in front of the girls.

"A pocketknife, a red bandanna, and a Hotel Saigon key chain with no keys," George said, examining the contents.

"And you never heard from Nick again?" Nancy asked.

"About a week after Nick went off on that mission, we heard that his unit had been hit by the North

18

Vietnamese Army. Eleven men were killed. Nick wasn't listed as one of them. There were rumors that the survivors were taken prisoner, but no one could ever prove that. They just disappeared. And after a few searches the army declared them MIA." Terry rubbed his eyes, suddenly looking exhausted. "Why don't we take this up again in the morning?" he asked. "I'm sorry, but I'm going to fall over if I don't get some sleep."

"Me, too," George said.

"And me," Bess added. "I need my beauty sleep."

"I think I'll stay up awhile," Nancy said.

A few minutes later Bess and George went upstairs to the second-floor room they were sharing with Nancy.

Nancy sat by the fireplace, staring into the dancing flames. She thought about the three break-ins and what had been stolen. The intruder could have been after any of the stolen items. But her mind kept circling back to the trunk. Terry said it wasn't worth anything. Its owner had disappeared years ago. And now the trunk itself was missing. Who wanted it? she wondered. And why?

The sun woke Nancy early the next morning. She lay in bed for a few moments, just enjoying the sight of the round window set high in the wall opposite her. Inside its wood frame was a stained-glass garland of blue and yellow forget-me-nots. Across the room from her George and Bess were still asleep. Careful not to wake them, Nancy got up and quietly dressed in jeans and a lavender-and-white striped rugby shirt.

Downstairs, she found Terry and Amy at the

19

kitchen table. "Good morning," Nancy said. "Have you heard from the police?"

"I called them this morning," Terry answered. "They told me what I already knew. Whoever broke in was a professional. He didn't leave any prints or any other clues. And the police have no record of any car like the dark red one that tore out of the driveway yesterday."

"What about your van?" Nancy asked.

"The tow truck should be arriving any minute now to pull it out of the ravine."

"Before it does, I'd like to take a look at the tire that blew," Nancy said.

"We might as well," Terry agreed. He and Nancy went outside, and Nancy had a chance to notice what she hadn't really seen the day before in all the confusion. Terry's house was surrounded by fragrant redwoods and eucalyptus. Wild jasmine and holly grew along the sides of the house, and far in the distance she could hear the sound of the Pacific breaking on the shore.

"How much of this is your property?" Nancy asked, gazing into the woods.

"I've got five acres surrounding the house," Terry answered. "Why?"

"I was just thinking that if someone was watching your house, waiting to see when you were out, they'd have plenty of places to hide."

"Wonderful," Terry muttered.

They reached the ravine and scrambled down to look at the tire. "It's pretty badly blown," Terry said. "It almost looks as if parts of it exploded."

"I don't think this happened from driving over

something sharp," Nancy said. She knelt and ran one hand along the remaining surface of the tire. Her heart started to pound as she felt a small, cold metal object embedded in the rubber. "I think I know what blew your tire," she said. "Do you have a pocket-knife? I'll have to dig it out."

Terry nodded and handed her a pocketknife.

Nancy applied it to the tire, and a few seconds later showed Terry what she had found. In her palm was a brass-colored bullet.

3

Stakeout

Terry took the bullet from Nancy's hand and gave a low whistle of astonishment. "It's been years since I've seen one of these."

"Do you recognize it?" Nancy asked.

"I don't think I could forget this if I tried," Terry said grimly. "It's from a Colt .45 1911-A1. We used them in 'Nam. But whoever fired it must have used a silencer. The only thing we heard was the sound of the tire blowing."

Nancy felt a chill run through her. "I'd say the man in the red car didn't want you to follow him. This may sound crazy, but did Nick Finney have light hair?"

"No," Terry answered, smiling at the memory. "Nick had fire-red hair. He was a little guy, no taller than you, but you couldn't miss him. In the field he always wore a hat or a bandanna. Otherwise, the enemy would have seen him miles away. In fact, he became very good at concealing himself."

Nancy pictured the light-haired man she saw in the car. Hair color can change, she thought, but the man behind the wheel had looked as if he had a large, solid build. If only she'd been able to get a better look.

Terry and Nancy returned to the house, where they found Bess and George in the kitchen, eating breakfast with Amy.

"We know what caused the blowout yesterday," Nancy said, showing them the bullet.

Bess choked on her oatmeal. "Someone shot out the tire?"

"It must have been whoever broke into the house," George said. "What about the man in the red car?"

"That's who I think it was," Nancy agreed. "But we still don't know what he was after. Or whether or not he actually found it."

Terry called the police again, to tell them about the bullet, and then called his insurance company. Finally he turned to his guests. "Look," he said, "when I invited you to stay here, my house had been broken into twice. But there weren't any guns or knives involved. Now things seem to be getting more dangerous. I'm not even sure Amy and I should be here. I think I should find you another place to stay."

Nancy's eyes met those of her friends. There was no question in her mind what George would say. She'd never known George to back off from a case. But Bess wasn't quite as brave, and Nancy didn't want to ask her friend to stay in a place that frightened her.

Bess met Nancy's gaze and then looked at Terry and Amy. "I think," she said, "that this is the most beautiful house I've ever seen, and I'm not going to let anyone scare me out of it."

"All right, Bess!" Amy cheered.

Terry raised his eyes up. "Okay," he said. "For now we all stay. But I don't like feeling as if I'm living in the middle of a target range. If anything else happens, I'm moving *everyone* to safer ground."

Later that afternoon, while Terry went to the police station to give them the bullet, Nancy, Bess, George, and Amy sat on the beach at Cherry Creek. Bess was working on her tan, and George and Amy were sorting through a collection of sand dollars. Nancy stared out at the Pacific, her mind still on the case. She was startled when Amy asked, "You're thinking about the break-ins, aren't you?"

Nancy helped herself to some of Bess's sunscreen. "How'd you guess?"

"I figured you were thinking about them because I am, too," Amy said.

"And?" Nancy asked, intrigued.

"And I've been thinking that every time our house was broken into, my dad and I were out."

"Thank goodness!" Bess exclaimed.

"Well, it was safer for us that way, but it means that someone's been watching the house," Amy said.

"And maybe still is," Nancy finished grimly.

Bess sat up straight. "Do you mean whoever broke in knows we're staying there?"

"He did see us drive up yesterday," George reminded her.

"I wonder how closely he was watching," Nancy said thoughtfully. "Unless someone else shot out the tire, the blond-haired man must have heard Terry's car approach, concealed himself in the woods, shot

24

out the tire, and then made his getaway. And it all happened pretty quickly." She gave Bess a reassuring smile. "Don't worry. If he is still watching the house, there may be a way we can turn the tables on him."

The girls returned to the house and saw that Terry's van had been pulled out of the ravine and the tire replaced. "Perfect," Nancy said. "Now if we can get Terry to cooperate, I think my plan will work."

Nancy found Terry in his studio, carefully molding a lead frame in the shape of a willow tree. "How was the beach?" he asked.

"Gorgeous," Nancy replied. "And so is that." She nodded toward his work. "Do you think I could convince you to leave the studio for a while?"

"Right now?" Terry asked reluctantly.

"If your house is still being watched by the thief, I want to set a trap," she explained. "But I'll need your help."

An hour later Terry, Amy, George, and Bess drove off. Sitting beside Terry in the van's front seat was a dressmaker's dummy they had found in the attic. The dummy wore a blond wig and Nancy's pale blue crewneck sweater. From a distance it looked like Nancy.

Nancy waited until they'd gone. She knew that if someone did break in again, remaining inside the house would be dangerous. So she very carefully let herself out through the door from Terry's studio. Then Nancy made her way through the trees so she could watch the house. Perched on a boulder beneath a majestic redwood, she began her stakeout.

The only sounds she heard were the wind chimes

that hung from the house and, in the distance, the Pacific breaking against the shore.

Waiting has got to be the most boring part of detective work, Nancy thought. And yet she knew she had to be patient. Occasionally she heard cars on the paved road, but none of them turned onto Terry's drive. The sun began to go down, and the air became cooler. Nancy began to shiver a little. She was still wearing the shorts and T-shirt she'd worn to the beach. And she was getting hungry. She drew her knees up to her chest and held herself close. And continued to wait.

A glimmer of movement at the edge of her vision made her start. Was it a deer? Or was someone watching *her?* Except for the birds calling, the woods were silent. Nancy decided to investigate. Carefully she moved through the trees, all her senses alert. She reached the spot where she thought she'd seen something. There were only trees and brush. Then something caught her eye—a torn scrap of flannel snagged on a prickly bush.

Nancy removed the plaid flannel from the bush. Someone *had* been here, she thought, her eyes sweeping the woods. From the spot where she stood she had a perfect view of the boulder she'd been sitting on. Someone had not only been here—he'd been watching her.

Nancy jumped as she heard a vehicle turning onto Terry's drive. Her heart began to race. As it approached, she realized it was Terry's van. He'd promised to return in two hours. The time was up.

The van pulled up in front of the house. "Any luck?" Terry called.

Nancy showed him the scrap of flannel and explained what had happened.

Terry's mouth tightened in a taut line. "Someone's still watching the house, and we didn't see him."

"What do you mean?" Nancy asked.

"We parked about a quarter of a mile away," George explained. "Then we all hiked to the other side of Terry's property just in case you needed backup."

"You mean you were here all along?" Nancy asked.

"Of course," Amy said. "Did you really think we'd let you take on the bad guys all by yourself?"

That evening Joanne Koslow and her fiancé, Keith, drove to the Kirklands'. When Bess had called her to say that she and her friends were staying with the Kirklands, Joanne had promptly invited Terry and Amy to the wedding and then invited herself and Keith for a visit.

Joanne had gotten much taller and thinner since Nancy had last seen her. She had the same straw-blond hair, but now she wore it very short. Joanne was the type of person who always stood out in a crowd, Nancy thought. Keith was quiet, with curly light brown hair and glasses.

"We're getting married in a barn," Joanne announced. "It's on this farm up on a hill overlooking the ocean. We've invited about three hundred people."

Bess's eyes grew wide. "Three hundred?" she repeated.

"It sounds wonderful," George said.

"I'm so glad you three are here," Joanne went on.

"The wedding is a week from tomorrow, and I thought I'd have most everything done by now. But I still need to make the casseroles, bake the cake, and get the decorations. I was thinking of silver bells with garlands of wildflowers. What do you think, Bess?"

Before Nancy knew it, Bess had promised Joanne that she, Nancy, and George would take care of the decorations. "We will?" Nancy murmured, wondering where she'd find the time, but no one seemed to notice.

Keith was so quiet that Nancy began to be very curious about him. When at last there was a lull in the discussion of wedding plans, Nancy managed to say, "Keith, are you a photographer, like Joanne?"

"Nothing that practical," Keith answered with a lopsided grin. "I'm in school, doing graduate work in Asian art history."

Nancy wondered briefly if Keith might know anything about the trunk from Vietnam, but before she could ask, Joanne was talking again.

"Keith's so lucky," she told them. "He gets to work with all these wonderful old scrolls and paintings. Two months ago we went to see an exhibit of antique silk kimonos, and I got the most fabulous idea. Guess what I'm wearing in the wedding?"

"A silk kimono?" Bess asked in disbelief.

"Just wait till you see it," Joanne said.

Nancy tried to picture a wedding in a barn with the bride in a kimono. George must have been doing the same, because she blinked her eyes, shook her head, and said, "So, Joanne, what have you been photographing lately?"

"Everything from mountain-climbing senior citizens to migrating whales. Some of the seniors are coming to the wedding."

"It's a wonder the whales aren't," Keith murmured.

By the time Joanne and Keith left that evening, Nancy, Bess, and George had a long list of decorations to buy. Nancy was glad to have a chance to help Joanne, but she knew that for her, the mystery would have to come first.

Early the next morning Nancy, Bess, and George got started on their shopping trip. Since Terry was going to one of his art shows, he took the van and gave the girls the use of his car. Amy elected to go with Nancy, Bess, and George.

The shopping trip lasted all day. Slowly the car trunk was filled with bags of ribbons and bells, candles and tablecloths, napkins and napkin rings, balloons and Oriental fans. Finally, Bess checked off the last item on the list and said, "That's it. We've got it all."

George uttered what sounded like a prayer of thanks, and the girls headed back to the Kirklands' house. As they drove, it began to rain.

"This rain is excellent," Amy said. "We've been having a drought. But our driveway's going to be a mess. The car won't be able to make it up. We'll have to park at the bottom of the hill and walk up to the house."

"No problem," said Nancy, who was driving. But what she hadn't counted on was how foggy the Cherry Creek area became in the rain. The dry, grassy hills vanished from sight, and even the huge redwoods were sucked into the soft white mist. Dusk

29

was falling. The only thing Nancy could see clearly was the stretch of road ahead of her illuminated by the car's headlights.

At last she turned onto the Kirklands' drive and parked the car at the bottom of the hill. As Amy had predicted, the driveway was a wash of mud. The rain was still coming down hard, so the girls decided to leave the packages in the car until it let up. They began the hike up the hill, George and Amy in the lead, followed by Bess.

Nancy was last. Rain streamed down her hair and into her eyes. In a matter of moments she was thoroughly soaked. I want my bathrobe and a mug of hot cocoa, Nancy thought. She was so busy imagining being warm and dry that she almost didn't notice the sound—the sound of someone running through the woods.

Nancy stopped, not believing anyone would really be out in this weather. Ahead of her, George, Amy, and Bess walked toward the house. Nancy peered into the dark, mist-cloaked trees. She couldn't see anything, but she could hear someone on her right breathing hard, scrambling down the muddy hill.

Cautiously Nancy moved toward the sound. And then a boy—he couldn't have been more than fifteen—broke out of the woods and raced onto the driveway.

"Stop!" Nancy shouted, taking off after him.

Neither one could move very fast on the muddy road. The boy was ahead of her, sliding. Nancy forced herself to go faster, then she lost sight of him as he disappeared into the woods on the other side of the drive.

Nancy stepped off the road and hesitated. The rain was still beating down in a steady rhythm, and the trees were shrouded in white mist. Then she heard the sound of an engine being kick-started and saw the light of a small headlamp. She ran toward it and reached the dirt bike just as the boy got on.

"Wait," she said, grabbing his arm.

The boy glared at her. She saw that he was Asian. His black hair was cut short on the sides and long in back, and a small silver dragon dangled from one ear. Up close he looked even younger than she had originally thought. "Let me go," he said angrily.

"Just tell me why you were running from the house," Nancy said. "Are you the one who's been breaking in?"

The boy shook her off and revved the bike's engine.

"Who are you?" Nancy demanded.

"Ask the kingfisher," said the boy with a sneer. Then he disappeared into the night.

4

The Kingfisher

Nancy listened as the thrum of the boy's dirt bike faded into the sound of the rain. Then, realizing that she was chilled, she made her way up to the house. Who was the boy? she wondered. And who or what was the kingfisher?

The lights were already on when Nancy reached the house. Once inside, she checked for signs of another break-in. Nothing had been touched.

She found George, Bess, and Amy in the kitchen, having a mild disagreement over what to have for dinner. Bess wanted to make a complicated casserole, George thought soup and sandwiches would be just fine, and Amy wanted to order out for Chinese food. Their conversation stopped when they saw Nancy.

"Did you just come in?" Bess asked. "I thought you were already upstairs, changing."

Nancy took off her soggy cardigan and pushed some

strands of wet hair out of her eyes. "Does the name *kingfisher* mean anything to you?"

"It's a bird," George replied. "Why? Don't tell me you were out there bird-watching in this weather."

"Not exactly," Nancy said. "When I was coming up the hill, I heard a noise in the woods. It was a teenage boy, and it looked as if he was running away from the house. I chased him to a dirt bike he'd left in the woods. And when I asked him what he'd been doing here, he said, 'Ask the kingfisher.' Then he took off."

"And you think he's our thief?" Bess asked.

"Not really," Nancy admitted. "He didn't look anything like the man in the dark red car, and he was too young to drive. Then again, maybe there has been more than one vandal."

"What did the boy look like?" Amy asked.

"He was about fourteen and Asian, with longish hair. He wore a silver dragon earring in one ear."

Amy's dark eyes widened at the description, but before Nancy could ask her if she knew the boy, the telephone rang and Amy went to answer it. "It's my dad," she reported after picking up the phone. "He says he won't be back until late tonight."

Nancy waited until Amy hung up. "Amy," she said, "do you know anyone who fits the description of the boy I saw tonight?"

Amy shook her head and glanced at the clock. "My favorite TV show is on—do you want to watch?"

"You'd better change into something dry," Bess told Nancy in a worried tone. "And take a hot shower. You're shivering."

"Yes, Mom," Nancy replied with a smile, but she went upstairs and took Bess's advice. As the hot water streamed down around her, Nancy's thoughts returned to the latest turn in the case. Who was the kingfisher? And how would she find him?

Later that evening, after Amy had gone to sleep, Nancy and her friends spread out in the living room with a phone book, a local newspaper, and a bird guide.

"All right," Nancy said in an official tone. "Your assignment is to find as much information as possible about kingfishers."

"It's definitely a bird," George reported as she flipped through the bird guide. "It's brightly colored with a short tail and a long, sharp bill. It dives for fish and then swallows them head first."

"Yuck," Bess said, looking up from the newspaper. "What am I supposed to be looking for, anyway? A column on birds?"

"Anything with the word *kingfisher* in it," Nancy replied. "Maybe *kingfisher* is the name of a local political leader . . . or a street gang. It could be anything. Just look for the word."

Bess skimmed the paper and soon announced that kingfishers simply were not in the news.

Nancy checked the phone book. She found no one with the last name of Kingfisher, and no stores or companies named after the bird. "This is driving me crazy," she said. "I set up a stakeout, and nothing happens—except *I* get watched. Then I get what may be our first real clue, and we all draw blanks. I don't even know if the boy is connected to the break-ins, or what it was the thief was looking for."

"Amy's sweaters?" George offered with a shrug.

"Right," Nancy said, smiling. "But somehow I've got a hunch that the trunk does have something to do with the mystery."

Nancy heard the sound of a key turning in the front door, and Terry walked in, looking exhausted. "What are you all doing up?" he asked. "Never mind, I'm beginning to recognize that gleam in Nancy's eye. You must be discussing the case."

"We got another clue tonight that led nowhere," Nancy said. Then she told him about the boy on the dirt bike. "Do you know anyone who fits that description?" she asked.

Terry shook his head. "No one I know, and Amy's friends are all much younger than him."

"What about the kingfisher?" Bess asked.

"Do we even have kingfishers in this area?" Terry asked. He dropped into a chair and closed his eyes, as if trying to travel back in memory. "Kingfisher, kingfisher. There's something familiar about that word." He sat up straight and opened his eyes. "Kingfisher is what they call jade in southeast Asia."

"You mean in Vietnam?" Nancy asked.

"And in Thailand and Burma. Over there jade is known as the 'feathers of the kingfisher.' You said the boy was Asian, so he might have known the term. Maybe you should be checking jewelry stores that sell jade."

"Finally," Nancy said, "something solid to go on." She turned to Bess and George, feeling happier than she'd been since the start of the case. "Why don't we call it a night?" she suggested. "Tomorrow we'll have lots of jewelry stores to call."

"That's twenty-seven jewelry stores that sell things made with jade and eighteen that don't," Bess said the next morning as she hung up the phone. "And none of them knew what I was talking about when I mentioned the kingfisher."

"Not true," George said. "Don't forget that nice man who invited you to go bird-watching with him."

Bess laughed and threw a pillow at her cousin.

Nancy took a last look at the phone directory and consulted her list. She, Bess, and George had spent the better part of the morning calling what had to be every jewelry store in northern California. And none of them had turned up anything. "Maybe there is no kingfisher," she said dejectedly. "Maybe that kid just said the most outlandish thing that came into his head, sure that I'd waste days trying to figure it out."

"Well," Bess said, stretching, "I say we all need a change of subject. I'm going to call Joanne and see about getting those decorations up to her house."

Nancy wasn't listening as Bess made the phone call. The more Nancy thought about things, the more frustrated she became. She just couldn't seem to make any progress on the case.

"Nancy, I've got Keith on the phone. I told him about our problem, and he wants to talk to you," Bess suddenly announced, jarring Nancy out of her thoughts.

Nancy took the phone, curious about what Joanne's boyfriend would have to say.

36

"Bess told me you were interested in jade," Keith began. "I'm not an expert, but I know that the finest green jade in the world comes from Burma. For the last seven hundred years the Chinese, the Thai, and everyone else in Southeast Asia have been trading for it. And Terry was right—they call it *fe t'sui*, or 'feathers of the kingfisher.'"

"Could you spell that for me?" Nancy asked.

Keith did, and after chatting for a few more minutes, Nancy hung up the phone. She walked over and looked through the phone book. "Here it is," she said, her voice low with amazement. "'Fe T'sui Gallery,'" she read, "'specialists in jade carvings. Sausalito.'"

George gave Bess a knowing grin. "Sounds like we're going to Sausalito today."

Bess looked worried. "We can't. I told Joanne we'd help her start decorating the barn today."

"Don't worry," Nancy broke in quickly. "You two can help Joanne. I can drop you off at her house, and then she can bring you back here when you're done."

Nancy called Joanne, who quickly agreed to the plan. When the three girls left, Terry was working in his studio and Amy was in school. Nancy drove Bess and George and the decorations to Joanne's house, then set off for Sausalito.

Nancy had seen Sausalito before when she'd solved a case involving one of Hannah Gruen's friends. But she was still charmed by the scenic town overlooking San Francisco Bay. She'd always wondered what it would be like to live there—either in one of the houses built into the cliffside or in one of the houseboats moored in the bay.

Glancing at the address she'd copied from the phone book, she passed Bridgeway, Sausalito's main street, and followed a series of side streets uphill.

Nancy found the Fe T'sui Gallery and parked the car a short distance away. As she entered the white stucco building, Nancy recognized the hushed atmosphere of an exclusive gallery. She could tell at once that the objects in the Fe T'sui were not for the average tourist who just happened to wander in. This was a gallery for serious collectors of jade.

A few people strolled among the display cases. Nancy did the same, taking mental notes on the gallery's clients. In the main room a heavyset man, wearing horn-rimmed glasses, stood studying a set of engraved jade tablets. Across from him a well-dressed couple viewed tiny carved animals.

A young blond-haired woman in an elegant sage-colored suit sat behind a mahogany desk. She nodded at Nancy, said, "Let me know if I can be of help," and then went back to reading through a file.

Nancy began to pay serious attention to the objects on display. The first thing she noticed was the wide variety of color in the stone. Nancy had always thought jade was green. Now she saw it could be milky white, spotted yellow, pale green, or a green so dark it was almost black.

Many of the pieces were from ancient China. There were jade amulets shaped like fish and frogs. The tiny statues were even more fantastic—elephants, horses, dragons, and even something that looked like a unicorn. Nancy found herself drawn to the more modern pieces. She especially liked a mirror and brush set made at the turn of the century. The handles were silver and the backs set with carved jade.

This is all wonderful, Nancy thought, but how is it connected to my case? She pictured the boy again, standing angry and defiant in the rain. She could almost hear him telling her to ask the kingfisher. Nancy had gotten the definite impression that the kingfisher was a person. If this gallery was where the boy had meant to send her, then she still needed to find the kingfisher himself.

Nancy went over to the woman behind the desk. "Excuse me," she said, "but are you the owner of the gallery?"

"No, that's Mr. Mai," the woman replied. "I'm afraid he's not here right now. Can I help you?"

Nancy thought quickly of Keith, then said, "I'm studying Asian art history, and I'm doing a paper on jade carvings. I was wondering if it would be possible to interview him."

The woman handed her a slip of paper. "Why don't you write down your name and number, and I'll have Mr. Mai get in touch with you."

Nancy didn't really expect Mr. Mai to call her, but she gave her name along with Terry's phone number. Then, thanking the woman, she left.

I'd better get to a library, Nancy thought. She would never pass as a student of Asian art history unless she did some research. But outside the sun was shining on the bay, and Nancy found she couldn't resist the impulse to spend at least a little time walking around Sausalito.

She decided to make her way down to the waterfront and look at the houseboats. Rounding the corner of the shop, she headed downhill toward the plaza. As she passed the back of the gallery building, she stopped. Behind it, on the street facing the water, was a small antique store, and between the two buildings was an alley.

Intrigued, Nancy entered the alley. It was empty except for several large wooden trash bins. Nancy saw empty cardboard boxes addressed to the Fe T'sui Gallery and wondered briefly if being a detective meant having to go through other people's garbage. And then she saw it, leaning against the farthest of the bins—the shattered remains of a small wooden trunk.

Nancy couldn't believe what she was seeing. Had she actually found Nick Finney's trunk? It looked as if someone had taken an ax to it.

She went over to the bin and picked up a slab of the shattered wood. She had just begun to examine the wood when she heard the sound of a low growl. Nancy dropped the wood and turned quickly, but not quickly enough. A powerfully built Doberman pinscher raced toward her and sprang, its open jaws aimed at her throat.

5

Trouble on Wheels

Nancy raised one arm to cover her face as she tried to dodge the vicious dog. She twisted to the side and felt its jaws clamp shut on the sleeve of her khaki jacket. Nancy pulled hard, trying to free herself. Growling furiously, the Doberman pulled back.

Fortunately, the jacket had loose, wide sleeves. The Doberman had the fabric, but it hadn't touched her arm. Nancy pulled again, desperately hoping the sleeve would tear and set her free before the Doberman decided to get a better grip on her.

"Ly!" Nancy heard someone shout. The dog stopped growling at the word but did not release her.

Nancy watched in amazement as the boy with the dragon earring strode toward her, an impatient look on his face. He gave the dog a sharp command in a language she didn't understand. The dog released her at once and sat on its haunches, clearly awaiting the

41

boy's next instruction. He spoke again, and the dog walked off calmly, as if the attack had never taken place.

"Are you hurt?" the boy asked Nancy.

"I don't think so," she answered, suddenly realizing how frightened she'd been. She looked at her jacket. Miraculously, it hadn't ripped. "No damage," she told him. "Is that your dog?"

He nodded, his gaze following the dog. "You'd better get out of here," he said in a flat tone. "Ly doesn't like strangers, and he's trained to attack."

"You told me to come here," Nancy argued. "You told me to ask the kingfisher."

"Forget what I said," the boy told her in the same emotionless voice.

"Is Mr. Mai the kingfisher?"

The boy gave her a grudging smile. "Very good. Now get out of here before I call the dog back."

"Tell me what you were doing at Terry Kirkland's house and I'll go," Nancy countered.

He didn't answer but gave a sharp, high whistle. Not again, Nancy thought as she saw the Doberman loping toward her. "All right," she said quickly. "I'm leaving."

The boy stared at her, his dark eyes hard. With the dog growling at his side, he led Nancy out of the alley, past the antique shop, and onto the street. "You're not only leaving," he said in a menacing tone, "you're never coming back."

This is ridiculous, Nancy thought. I'm taking orders from a fourteen-year-old! But the dog gave her no choice.

Feeling annoyed, Nancy headed once again toward

the center of town. There she bought a sandwich and found a grassy spot to sit near the water's edge.

As she watched the sailboats skim across the bay, Nancy tried to piece together what she'd learned. She now knew that Mr. Mai was the kingfisher and definitely connected to the trunk. Was the boy also connected to its theft? If he was, why would he have sent her here? And how did he connect to the kingfisher?

The more Nancy thought about the trunk, the more she knew it was critical to unraveling the mystery. She wondered if its pieces were still where she'd seen them, or if the boy had removed them. Nancy finished her lunch and made a decision that she didn't particularly like. She was going to have to go back for the trunk.

Nancy's pulse was racing well before she even reached the alley. Would the boy and the dog be waiting for her? Nancy had risked many dangerous things as a detective, but even she had to admit that chancing a second run-in with an attack-trained Doberman was among the craziest.

She reached the antique shop, began to turn up the alley, and hesitated. I can't do it, she realized. She just couldn't walk in the alley unprotected and take on the Doberman. Then she remembered something she'd seen the day before when she, Bess, and George had been shopping for Joanne's wedding decorations.

Excitedly she returned to the car and opened the trunk. There it was, just as she'd remembered, an old comforter, which Terry must have kept in the car as a spare beach blanket. It was worn and badly faded but still fairly thick. It was exactly what she needed.

Nancy got into the car and drove to the antique shop. Taking the comforter with her, she returned to the alley. She wrapped the quilt around her arm and slowly approached the garbage bins. The shattered trunk was still there.

She heard the dog's warning growl as she reached for the first piece of wood. "Just ignore him," she told herself.

But moments later the dog sprang, and this time Nancy went down under its weight. Pushing her protected arm toward the Doberman's mouth, Nancy struggled to get up.

The dog's teeth sank into the quilt. It pulled savagely at the comforter while Nancy reached into the bin with her other arm and grabbed as much of the shattered wood as she could. Then, after slipping her arm out of the quilt, she ran as if she'd never stop.

Nancy jumped into the front seat of Terry's car, slammed the door, and exhaled a sigh of relief. Waiting for her pulse to slow down, she looked beside her on the front seat at the pieces of wood she'd managed to salvage. In the first moments after she'd slipped her arm from the quilt, the dog had continued to chew on the thick cloth. That had given her the precious seconds she'd needed to outrun it. She shook her head as she recalled her panicked race to the car and her frantic struggle to open the door and lock herself safely inside.

She checked her watch. She'd been sitting in the car for over five minutes and her heart was still beating rapidly. Nancy glanced at the pieces of wood on the seat beside her. "I sure hope that was worth all this trouble," she said. Then she started the car and headed back to Cherry Creek.

She found Terry still in his studio, assembling a delicate glass mobile. He looked up and brushed a shock of long hair back from his face as she entered. "Any luck with the kingfisher?" he asked.

"I'm not sure *luck* is the word," Nancy replied, thinking of her run-in with the dog. "But I did find these."

Terry took the broken pieces of wood from her. "These look like they're from Nick's trunk."

"That's what I thought," Nancy said, then told him what had happened.

Terry listened to the story silently. "What I'd like to know is why this trunk wound up in pieces behind the gallery, and what that kid with the dog has to do with it."

Nancy sat down on a chair. "The first time I saw him I asked if he was the one who was breaking into your house, and he told me to ask the kingfisher. This time he pretty much admitted that the kingfisher was Mr. Mai. And I found pieces of the trunk behind Mai's gallery."

Terry frowned. "I think we can assume the kid knows who took the trunk. But there's something off about his story. He sounds too eager to blame Mai. Besides, owners of exclusive galleries usually have better things to do than steal worthless trunks."

"What if Mai paid him to steal it?"

Terry gave her a skeptical look. "That trunk was nailed together from cheap wood in a factory in Saigon. It wasn't worth anything. No one would bother to have it stolen. Especially someone who deals in real art."

"That brings us back to the boy and the man in the dark red car," Nancy said. "Maybe they're working together."

"And trying to frame Mr. Mai?" Terry asked.

"I don't know," she admitted. "I still don't have enough information." She nodded toward the remnants of the trunk. "Do you think that will tell us anything?"

Altogether Nancy had managed to bring back nine pieces of various sizes. Terry cleared a space on his worktable, laid out the pieces of wood side by side, and studied them intently. "I wish you'd been able to get more of it," he said at last. "But leave them with me for a while, and I'll see what I can figure out."

"And I'd better get to a library," Nancy said. "I want a list of halfway intelligent questions I can ask Mr. Mai if he calls back."

It was early evening when Nancy left the library with a pad filled with notes on Asian jade. She'd learned that there were basically two types of jade: jadeite, which was often translucent; and nephrite, which usually had a waxy quality. The oldest, most valuable carved pieces were generally from China. And the Burmese, Thai, Vietnamese, and Japanese all valued the stone as a symbol of good fortune. They had all used it to create beautiful works of jewelry and art.

She walked out of the library just as the sun was beginning to set. Perfect timing, Nancy thought. One of the things she loved about northern California was the way so many people pulled off the road at sunset to watch the sun go down over the Pacific. As Joanne had once told her, "It's definitely the best show in town."

Nancy got into her car and headed for Route 1. She had noted an overlook on the way to Cherry Creek that would be a perfect place to view the sky.

She followed the winding, wooded road along Mount Tamalpais, enjoying the turns that suddenly revealed views of the rugged coastline. Soon she saw a sign for the overlook she wanted. It was just ahead.

Nancy signaled that she wanted to turn off the road and checked her rearview mirror. Her first reaction to what she saw was a surge of irritation. Some crazy driver was tailgating her, riding so close he was nearly on her rear bumper. Then she looked again. Her blood ran cold as she realized who was following so closely. Directly behind her was the fair-haired man in the dark red car.

6

A Secret Revealed

Nancy studied the driver in her rearview mirror. He wore dark sunglasses, but she had no doubt that he was the same man who'd shot out the tire on Terry's van and had probably ransacked the house.

She glanced ahead at the turnout. There was one other car parked there, but Nancy couldn't count on the other car for help. She saw that there was no guardrail between the steep cliff and the trees below. She couldn't risk having the fair-haired man send her over the edge. Somehow she'd just have to shake him.

Nancy accelerated, knowing that neither car could go as fast on the twisting mountain road without disastrous results. Behind her, the dark red car sped up. It was larger than Terry's car and probably had a more powerful engine. Nancy had a sickening feeling that if the chase became a matter of speed, she wouldn't have a chance.

All right, then, she thought, silently challenging the man in the dark red car, I'll just have to outsmart you. What she needed was a way off the highway that didn't involve a crash.

The two cars sped along the road and over the crest of Mount Tamalpais. Nancy began the descent, worried because the chase was becoming increasingly faster. Still, she knew there were a number of exits nearby. She'd have her chance to get off the highway soon. Then what will I do? she asked herself. And then she remembered an old trick her father had taught her.

Nancy took the first exit she saw. The man in the dark red car followed closely behind. Night was falling. They were on a road leading toward the ocean and what Nancy hoped would be a town. Ahead of her the road cut through miles of low, grassy hills.

The road had forked, and Nancy veered to the left. Her spirits sank as she saw that there were no houses in sight, only another long, deserted stretch of dark road. She stiffened as her body jerked forward against the seat belt. The blond-haired man had hit her rear bumper. She gasped as he hit her again, this time much harder. He's trying to push me off the road, Nancy realized.

Nancy pressed all the way down on the gas pedal, pulling away from the dark red car. She drove farther into the darkness and finally saw what she'd been hoping for. Ahead were buildings with lights. She'd found a town. Now if only I can reach it before this maniac does serious damage, she thought.

She felt another hard jerk, and the front end of her

49

car skittered to the right. Nancy fought to control the wheel. She veered onto the dirt shoulder but pulled the car back onto the road just as it curved into the main street of town.

At last Nancy saw what she wanted just ahead of her. Thanks for the idea, Dad, she thought as she drove into the one place she knew the fair-haired man wouldn't follow—the parking lot of the local police station. As she pulled into a parking spot, she saw the red car go speeding by.

Inside the police station Nancy filed a report with a police officer who was much more helpful than Detective Brower had been. Officer Harlan took a report and alerted patrol cars to watch for the dark red car. Then he followed Nancy back to Cherry Creek just in case the fair-haired man was waiting.

By the time Nancy arrived at Terry's, she was exhausted. Bess and George were in the living room watching TV when Nancy walked in the door. "Are you all right?" George asked at once.

"Not exactly," Nancy admitted. "I just had one of the worst rides of my life. And the afternoon wasn't too terrific, either." She settled herself on the rug and gratefully accepted a mug of hot cider from Bess. Then she told her friends what had happened that day.

Bess looked confused. "Does that mean the man in the red car followed you to the library?"

"I've been wondering about that," Nancy said. "But I think that if he was following me all day, he'd have done something in Sausalito when I was going after the pieces of the trunk."

"Maybe the boy with the dog works for him,"

George suggested. "Maybe the boy told him about you."

"That's possible," Nancy said doubtfully, "but I think it's more likely it was coincidence. I think he might have been near the library and recognized Terry's car."

"And he may have recognized you," Bess added. "Remember, he might have been the one watching during your stakeout."

Nancy felt her head spinning with possibilities. All she knew for certain was that the fair-haired man had tried to kill her. "So," she said, changing the subject, "how did the decorating go?"

"Wait until you see the barn," Bess said. "We put up all the decorations, and it's gorgeous!"

"All of them?" Nancy asked in disbelief.

"*All* of them," George assured her wearily. "But it really is beautiful. The property is right beside the ocean, and the barn sits on top of this high, grassy hill. You can see right down to the water."

The door to Terry's studio opened, and Amy stuck her head out. "Come inside, all of you," she called. "You've got to see what my dad's done."

The three friends trooped into Terry's studio. Nancy expected to see another glass creation. Instead, the object on Terry's workbench was an odd wooden thing, tilting at a very unstable angle.

Nancy stared at it for a moment, puzzled, then her face lit with recognition. "You reconstructed the trunk from the pieces I brought you."

"Part of it, anyway," Terry said. "It's just held together with glue. It's pretty fragile."

"That's Nick Finney's trunk?" Bess asked.

"Well, the brass fittings are missing." Terry pointed to places where the brass had been stripped. "But as far as Amy and I can tell, that's his trunk all right—almost half of it."

"And more than we thought," Amy added mysteriously.

Her father winked at her. "Show 'em, pumpkin."

Amy gently lifted the trunk and set it on its side so that the girls could see its base. She slid out the panel of wood that had been the bottom of the trunk.

Nancy felt her eyes widen. "The trunk had a false bottom!"

"All along," Terry said. "I had that thing for years, and I never noticed."

Nancy examined the reconstructed trunk carefully. "Usually, the reason to use a false bottom is to transport something that you don't want anyone else to know about."

"You mean to smuggle something across a border?" Bess asked.

"Exactly," Nancy said. "The secret compartment could be used for something stolen or something illegal or else something very valuable that the owner wanted to protect."

George ran a hand through her short, dark hair. "Do you think that there was something hidden in the trunk all along?"

Nancy nodded. "That's what I'm guessing. The trunk has always been a hiding place. And someone who knew what was in it broke into the house and stole it."

"Not necessarily," Terry pointed out. "It could

have been taken by someone who wasn't sure what was inside. And we don't know that the thief actually found anything. For all we know, the hidden compartment was empty."

"No way, Dad," Amy said.

"You had no idea the trunk had a false bottom?" Nancy asked Terry.

"Not until ten minutes ago."

"How about you, Amy?"

She shook her dark head. "I would have used it for my jewelry if I knew."

"So," Nancy concluded, "the question is, who *did* know about the secret compartment?"

There was silence in the studio, and then Terry sighed. "There's at least one answer to that," he said quietly. "Nick Finney."

"That's who I come up with, too," Nancy said. "Did Nick ever—"

"Excuse me," Terry said as the phone rang. He picked up the receiver, listened, then handed it to Nancy. "For you. Mr. Mai."

Surprised, Nancy took the phone.

"Ms. Drew," said a cultured voice with a slight accent. "This is Binh Mai of the Fe T'sui Gallery. You wanted to speak with me?"

"Yes," Nancy said. "I'm a student majoring in Asian art history, and I'm doing a paper on jade carvings. I was hoping I could interview you."

Mr. Mai hesitated. "I'm sorry, Ms. Drew, but I'm a very busy man, and I'm afraid I don't have the time to meet with you."

"I won't take up much of your time," Nancy said

quickly. "It's just that I've heard your gallery has one of the finest collections in the area, and that your expertise—"

Mr. Mai sighed and interrupted her. "Very well. Come Tuesday at eleven-fifteen. I can give you exactly forty minutes." He hung up before she had a chance to accept.

"You're going to see Mr. Mai?" Bess asked.

"Tomorrow morning."

"Maybe one of us should go with you," George suggested.

Nancy smiled at her loyal friend. "Thanks," she said, "but if Mr. Mai is involved with the thefts, I don't want to make him suspicious. It's better if I go on my own."

"He may also get a visit from the police," Terry said. "I called Brower and told him about the trunk. He and his technician will be by in the morning to have a look."

"What a way to start the day," Bess said. "A visit from Detective Brower."

Much later that evening Nancy curled up beside the fireplace with a mystery novel. Bess and George had gone to a movie she had already seen. Amy was asleep, and Terry was still in his studio, trying to finish a piece for his next show.

Nancy had almost finished the book when Terry came out of his studio. "I need a break," he said. "And you wanted to ask me about Nick Finney. Let's go outside for a few minutes."

Nancy put on a sweater and followed Terry onto one of the decks that surrounded the house. She took a deep breath of fir-scented air. Above them the winter stars shone through a canopy of redwoods.

"It sure is beautiful here," Nancy said.

Terry smiled. "I've always liked it. And I thought it was a safe place for my family, but the things that have been happening lately make me wonder."

"Terry, if Nick knew about the false bottom on the trunk, do you think he hid something in there? Maybe that's why your house was broken into three times— the intruder was looking for the trunk all along."

Terry gazed out into the darkness. "Maybe."

"I know this sounds crazy," Nancy went on, "but is it also possible that Nick is the one who stole the trunk, that he wanted his property back?"

"No," Terry said, "it's not. First of all, Nick disappeared over twenty years ago in the middle of an enemy attack. You're talking about someone coming back from the dead. And even if by some miracle he were alive, he wouldn't have had to break into my house to get his own trunk. All he had to do was ask. I'd have gladly given it back to him."

Nancy had no answer for that. Instead, she asked, "What else do you know about Nick?"

Terry shrugged. "He was a good soldier. He was especially good at things like concealing himself and following other people."

"What do you know about his disappearance?"

"Nothing more than I already told you. But you might try calling the local veterans' group. Nick originally came from this area, so they might have some records on him. I can give you the number."

"Great. I'll try them in the morning." Nancy

headed back into the house, leaving Terry staring into the trees. "Good night," she said. "And thanks."

Early the next morning, before Amy left for school, Detective Brower and the technician returned. Terry led them into the studio and showed them the reconstructed trunk. The technician took photographs.

Detective Brower just stared. At last he glanced at the technician and said, "Dust it for prints. Then I want you to take prints from Kirkland, Ms. Drew here, and the kid." He glanced at Bess and George. "Did either of you handle it?"

Bess and George both said they hadn't touched the trunk. Nancy, Terry, and Amy all had their fingerprints taken.

"We're going to take the trunk with us as evidence," Brower said. "We'll let you know when you can have it back."

"Are you going to check out the Fe T'sui Gallery?" Nancy asked the detective.

Brower ignored her. "I'll let you know what we find," he told Terry.

"That man has no manners!" Bess cried when Brower and the technician were gone.

George agreed. "He makes you want to solve the case first, just to irritate him."

Nancy smiled. "We may just have to do that. I'd better get started—I'm going to call the veterans' group."

Nancy made the call. But when she asked about Nick Finney, she was told that they didn't have any information. Instead, she was given another number to call.

After five such phone calls Nancy finally reached someone who was able to pull the soldier's record. She asked for his date of birth and the date when he was declared missing, then did some quick subtraction. "He was only eighteen when he disappeared?" she asked.

"That's right," the man said.

"Is there anything else?" Nancy asked. "Has anyone heard from him since he vanished?"

There was the sound of a computer keyboard in the background, and then the man's reply. "He was on a classified mission. Eleven men died, Finney not among them. Our government looked into the possibility that he was taken prisoner of war. . . . I'm sorry, there isn't anything else."

Still Nancy wouldn't give up. "When someone's been missing that long," she said, "what do you generally think has happened to them?"

The man hesitated. "Did you know Finney personally?"

"No," Nancy said.

"He's not a relative of yours?"

"No."

"All right, then," the man continued. "Let me be completely honest with you. Considering where that boy was and when, you could bet money on the fact that Nicholas Finney has been dead for years."

7

Quicksilver

Nancy sat in the kitchen, staring at the telephone receiver. She was eighteen, the same age Nick Finney had been when he disappeared. She shuddered as she tried to imagine what might have befallen the young soldier in the jungles of Vietnam.

She went upstairs and changed into a white button-down blouse, a denim vest, and a denim skirt for her interview with Mr. Mai. "Do I look like someone studying Asian art?" Nancy asked as Bess came into the room behind her.

Bess frowned. "Not particularly, but you do look like a student. Maybe you could wear some Oriental jewelry."

"I don't have any," Nancy said, putting on a pair of small turquoise earrings. "I guess these will have to do. What are you and George doing today?"

"Casseroles," Bess replied.

"Eggplant, crab, apple, spinach, and turkey, just for

starters," George added, coming into the room. "And what I really want to do is rent mountain bikes and go trail riding."

"I want to go up to Calistoga and take a mud bath," Bess said wistfully.

Nancy looked at her friends with concern. "This trip isn't turning out to be much fun for you, is it?"

"Actually," George said, "we're having a lot of fun hanging out with Joanne. I just wish we could do something besides work on wedding preparations. If I ever get married, I'm definitely eloping."

"No, you're not," Bess said. "I insist on going to your wedding and making sure you get the right wedding dress. Aren't you glad I picked out the green one you're wearing to Joanne's wedding?"

George rolled her eyes. Nancy laughed and said, "You'll get a break soon, I promise. Terry has an art show tomorrow, and since Amy's school has the day off for a teacher's conference, we can all go."

"I still think one of us should go to the gallery with you," George said.

Nancy shook her head. "No, I don't want to make Mr. Mai suspicious. I've got to do this on my own."

At eleven o'clock Nancy parked outside the Fe T'sui Gallery. Just to be prepared, she took one last look at the notes she'd taken in the library. At a quarter after eleven she entered the gallery.

Again she was greeted by the young blond woman at the mahogany desk.

"Is Mr. Mai here?" Nancy asked. "I have an appointment with him."

The young woman took her name, made a phone

call, and then told Nancy that Mr. Mai would be with her in a few minutes. Nancy took advantage of the wait and had another look around. No one else was in the gallery, she noted, and the display hadn't changed since the day before. An intricately carved statue of a dragon with one claw raised high caught her attention.

"So you like my dragon?" The smooth voice at her elbow surprised Nancy, and she turned with a start.

Behind her stood a man wearing a perfectly tailored pearl-gray suit. He was about an inch taller than she was, and powerfully built.

"Mr. Mai?" Nancy asked.

The man nodded slightly. "Do you like my dragon?" he repeated.

"It's beautiful," Nancy said.

"In Buddhism the dragon represents the god of the East," Mr. Mai explained. "He is the spirit of change —some say of life itself—and the lord of all sea creatures. Just as the tiger, the god of the West, represents courage and is lord of all land creatures. The piece you are looking at is from eighteenth-century Japan."

Nancy studied Mr. Mai as he spoke, but she couldn't tell how old he was. With his high cheekbones and jet black hair, he could have been thirty or fifty. The only thing certain was that he had money. Everything from his elegant suit to the antique jade ring on his hand was obviously expensive.

He nodded toward a case that held the inscribed tablets of jade she'd noticed yesterday. "This is what we call a jade book. The writing is actually a poem from the Manchu Dynasty. Jade books were something of a fad among the Chinese emperors of that period. Which period are you focusing on, Ms. Drew?"

That's a good question, Nancy thought. Somehow, when she'd done her research at the library, she hadn't thought too specifically about different periods in history. What she wanted to do was find out what might have been in the trunk.

"Actually," Nancy said, "it isn't a specific period I'm interested in. I'm researching jade carvings from Vietnam." At once she wondered if she'd said the wrong thing. There *might* have been a piece of jade in the trunk, but the jade itself could have come from anywhere in Southeast Asia.

"I was born in Vietnam," Mr. Mai said. "Many of the jade carvings from my country were done in the last two centuries. A great many were statues made for the temples."

"Do you have any here?" Nancy asked.

"Nothing at the present," Mr. Mai said. "I'm afraid I can't help you."

With a sinking feeling, Nancy realized the interview was over and she'd learned nothing about Mr. Mai except that he was Vietnamese. And that wasn't enough to tie him to the trunk. She glanced at the heavy wooden door behind him. What she really wanted was to get into the back room of the gallery. That was probably where new shipments were unpacked and where the displays were set up.

"Mr. Mai," Nancy said, thinking quickly of a way to

61

prolong the interview, "aren't many of the Vietnamese carvings similar to the Chinese?"

"Some of those that were made for the Buddhist temples are," he answered.

"Do you have anything here like that?"

For the next twenty minutes Mr. Mai gave Nancy a tour of his gallery. He was clearly an expert on his subject and lectured at a rapid speed.

Knowing she had to keep her cover as a student, Nancy took notes, but most of the information on jade flew past her. Instead, she listened for something that would link Mr. Mai or the gallery to the trunk.

It didn't take long before Nancy realized that the reason Mr. Mai had agreed to see her was that he was a very vain man. He knew a tremendous amount about his subject and was running a very successful business. And he liked lecturing to people about what he'd accomplished.

Nancy decided her best strategy was to act extremely impressed. "Where do you find all these amazing pieces?" she asked after he'd shown her a vase from sixteenth-century China.

Mr. Mai smiled for the first time since she'd met him. "Private collectors," he replied. "This is a highly specialized field. Most of the jade collectors know each other. We're a very small circle."

Nancy was running out of questions. She couldn't think of anything that would prompt him to show her more of the gallery—particularly the back room. And then the door to the back room slowly opened.

Casually Nancy stepped to the side so that she could get a glimpse of what was behind the door. But her eyes never got as far as the room itself. Standing in the open doorway was the boy with the silver dragon earring.

The boy's eyes met hers, and without a word he turned and bolted.

"Stop!" Nancy shouted. She knew she couldn't let him get away again, not when he seemed to be the key to the mystery.

"Ms. Drew!" Mr. Mai yelled out.

Nancy had no time to explain. She took off after the boy, racing past file cabinets and display cases. The boy obviously knew where he was going. He moved deftly through the back room, around a corner, and through a door that led out of the gallery.

Nancy followed him and found herself in the alley behind the gallery. Praying that she wouldn't have a third encounter with the Doberman, she continued to chase the boy out of the alley and into the streets of Sausalito.

The boy sprinted downhill toward the bay, his arms pumping as he sped along a narrow street. Nancy followed as quickly as she could, but she was wearing a skirt and couldn't run at her usual speed.

Her breath was coming in short gasps by the time the boy reached the Plaza Vina del Mar. He skirted the fountain, nearly collided with an elderly man, then darted around one of the plaza's elephant statues and disappeared.

Nancy slowed to a halt and eyed the plaza in disbelief. Where could he have gone? she asked herself. He couldn't have just vanished. He had to be somewhere nearby.

Patiently she began to search the plaza and Gabrielson Park. But there was no trace of a boy in a white T-shirt and black jeans who wore a silver dragon earring.

Who *is* he? she wondered. And what is he so desperate to hide?

8

Back from the Grave

With a sigh Nancy sat down next to one of the plaza's elephant statues. She'd lost the boy with the silver dragon earring. What was he doing inside the gallery, anyway? she wondered. He'd clearly been alarmed when she saw him. Did he work there? Or was he about to steal something?

Nancy reviewed what she knew about the boy. She'd first seen him at Terry's house, and he'd sent her to the gallery. Then she'd seen him behind the gallery with his dog and had just seen him again inside the gallery. That meant there was a good chance he lived in Sausalito. Her next step would be to ask some of the local storekeepers and business people if they knew him. After all, she reasoned, he was easy to recognize.

But first she had to get back up the hill and explain her mad race through the gallery to Mr. Mai. And she had no idea of what she'd tell him.

Nancy approached the gallery and peered through the window. Mr. Mai was standing near the entry, talking to the woman at the desk. Hesitantly Nancy went back in.

Mr. Mai turned to face her, and she saw at once that her task was not going to be easy. The gallery owner wore a cold, closed expression. "Ms. Drew," he said with a nod, "you left very suddenly."

"I saw someone I thought I recognized," Nancy said.

"Do you always chase people you think you recognize?" Mr. Mai inquired.

"No," Nancy answered, feeling her face flush with embarrassment. "Was the boy someone you know?"

"Jimmy is my nephew," Mr. Mai replied. "He lives with me above the gallery. I am his legal guardian."

Nancy sat down on one of the gallery's leather sofas and tried to take the news in. "I'm sorry," she said. "He saw me and ran. I assumed it was because he was trying to steal something."

"That is a very unkind assumption," Mr. Mai noted.

Nancy wished that the couch would open up and swallow her. She wished she'd never returned to the gallery. "I'd—I'd like to apologize to him," she said.

"He won't talk to you," Mr. Mai said. "My nephew lacks certain social graces. He's an orphan, you see. His parents were killed in Vietnam shortly after his seventh birthday."

"In the war?"

"I suppose you could say that, although technically the war was over. His parents drove over a land mine. The mine was probably waiting there for years. As you can imagine, Jimmy found his parents' deaths rather upsetting."

Nancy noticed that whenever Mr. Mai spoke of Jimmy, his voice took on a tone of cool distaste, as if he were discussing a piece of inferior art.

"The boy has been extremely rebellious ever since," the gallery owner went on. "It seems my nephew's greatest talent is getting into trouble. So far I'm the fourth relative to take him in. He's not an easy child."

He's not a *wanted* child, Nancy thought, feeling an unexpected surge of sympathy for the boy. She was glad she'd never had to live with a guardian who discussed her with such contempt.

Mr. Mai looked impatiently at his watch. "I've already given you more time than I planned, Ms. Drew. I'm afraid I have other commitments."

"Of course," Nancy said, getting up to go. But inside she knew she had to return to the gallery. Now that she knew that Jimmy was Mr. Mai's nephew, she was more sure than ever that there was a connection between Mr. Mai and the stolen trunk. "Would it be possible to come back later this week?" she asked. "I just have a few more questions on the temple carvings."

Mr. Mai gave her a look of annoyance but said grudgingly, "Very well." He held out his hand, and the woman sitting at the desk handed him a large black leather appointment book. "The day after tomorrow, ten A.M. sharp," he told Nancy.

"Thank you. I appreciate it," Nancy said. "I'll see you then."

* * *

Nancy had arranged to meet Bess and George at Joanne's after her appointment with Mr. Mai. She entered Joanne's house to find every table and counter in sight covered with trays, pans, and casserole dishes. Bess, George, and Joanne sat in the living room, checking off items from a list on the coffee table.

"We did it!" Joanne announced proudly as she reached the end of the list. "We have food for three hundred people."

"This looks fantastic," Nancy said. "You guys should open a restaurant."

Bess took a cracker from a tray. "That's not a bad idea," she said, munching thoughtfully.

"Don't even think about it," George said.

Joanne took off her apron. "I'm with George," she said heartily. "After this week Keith and I eat out."

"Where's your family?" Nancy asked Joanne. "I was looking forward to seeing them again."

"You'll see them at the wedding," Joanne promised. "Today I sent them to the Exploratorium in the city. They were driving me up the wall. My mother kept asking why I couldn't get married in a nice little catering hall like everyone else."

"She hasn't changed," Nancy observed. When Joanne was in junior high, Mrs. Koslow was always asking why her daughter couldn't dress like everyone else.

"My mom never changes," Joanne said, laughing. "Here, I'll show you a picture."

"You know, I don't think I've ever seen any of Joanne's photographs," Nancy said as Joanne went to find the picture.

"They're great," George said. "Bess and I looked through her portfolio yesterday. Wait till you see the ones of the whales."

Joanne appeared a few minutes later carrying a large brown envelope. "Here," she said, settling down on the couch and handing Nancy a stack of photographs. "I took these while my mom and sisters were out here last summer. And the ones at the end are from that kimono exhibit I went to with Keith." She pointed to a picture of a mannequin dressed in a luxurious green-and-gold silk kimono. "That's the one I really wanted to get married in. Unfortunately, it's worth about thirty thousand dollars and belongs to a museum in Japan."

Nancy stared at the photograph of the kimono, an idea forming in her mind. "Where was this photograph taken?" she asked.

"It's a small gallery in Berkeley," Joanne answered. "The minute I saw those kimonos, I knew I wanted photographs as inspiration for my wedding kimono. So I went back with my tiny pocket camera and just snapped away."

"I thought galleries didn't like that," Bess said. "Didn't anyone notice you?"

Joanne grinned. "I made Keith come with me and distract the curator with art-student questions."

Nancy stared at the photograph, noting how sharp and perfect it was. I'd love to get photographs like this of the carvings in Mr. Mai's gallery, she thought. "Joanne," she said, "I know you're caught up in wedding preparations, but do you think you could go on an hour's photo shoot with me the day after tomorrow?"

"That's Thursday," Joanne said, "the day I'm baking the cake."

"You're baking your own wedding cake?" Nancy asked in disbelief.

"And we're helping," Bess said. "All three of us. The cake is going to look like a medieval castle. You'll see. It will be great."

"I'd be happy to help with the cake on Thursday," Nancy said, "but I've got to go see Mr. Mai at ten in the morning. Is there any chance you could bring your little camera and come with me?"

Joanne thought for a moment, then said, "I'll help you with your case, and you'll help me with my cake. That sounds like a fair trade to me. Just let me know where you want me to meet you."

Shortly after dawn on Wednesday Nancy and her friends helped Terry and Amy load the van with Terry's work. Still half asleep, they all piled into the van and set off for the art show, which was in the northernmost part of the state, just below the Oregon border.

Hours later Terry pulled up in front of an octagonal redwood building. A large sign read A Gathering of Glassworkers—Fifty of Today's Finest Artists—Open to Dealers Only.

"Sounds good, Dad," Amy said from the back of the van. "They think you're one of the fifty finest."

"What they actually mean is that I'm one of fifty artists who were willing to drive all the way out here in the middle of the week," her father replied. He pulled into the parking lot, and he and the girls began the slow and careful process of unloading. Nancy and George teamed up to carry a display table while Bess brought in a stack of printed sheets that listed all of Terry's pieces and their prices. Amy took charge of the notebook for writing down orders. Terry carried in all of the glasswork.

The area that Terry had been assigned for his display was at the edge of the large open hall, near the back. Nancy was sure that setting up the various windows, lamps, and mobiles would take hours. But Terry had done it many times before, and within half an hour everything was in place.

Amy removed the wrappings from an iridescent glass box and handed it to her father. "Your table looks excellent," she told him.

"My biggest fan," Terry said fondly. "Let's hope the dealers agree with you."

"You're being modest, Kirkland." A gray-haired man in a dark blue suit approached the booth and shook hands with Terry. "You're one of the main reasons that I and half the dealers here showed up today."

Terry introduced the man as Leon Isaacs, owner of a New York gallery. Isaacs immediately pointed to one of the mobiles and asked for its price.

"Come on," said Amy, who was a veteran of other art shows. "It's going to be like this all day. We might as well walk around."

While Terry had set up his display, the other artists had been setting up theirs. Now there were three aisles filled with booths. Sunlight poured in from the large rectangular windows above, illuminating the glasswork. Deep ruby reds and sapphire blues, soft lavenders and palest pinks, greens and ambers caught the light, shimmering.

"All these colors," Bess gasped. "It looks like one of those rooms in a fairy tale. You know, the rooms that hold all the jewels in the kingdom."

"It's just glass," Amy said.

"But it's amazing," George said. She stopped to peer at a statue of a woman made of glass. "She looks so real, I'd swear I saw her breathing a minute ago."

"That's because this show is for the best glass workers," Amy said proudly.

The four girls wandered the hall until it was nearly lunchtime. Terry had told them that they could take the van any time they'd had enough of the art show. There were redwood forests nearby, and it was a good day for a hike.

"I think we ought to bring your dad some lunch and then take a ride," Nancy told Amy. Bess, George, and Amy agreed to the plan, and they made their way through the crowded floor back to Terry's exhibit.

Terry was standing outside his booth with his back to them. "What's he doing over there?" Amy asked. "He should be on the other side of the table."

Instinct told Nancy that something was wrong, and as she neared Terry, she saw she was right. The delicate box made of iridescent glass that had sat proudly on a black velvet platform at the very center of the table now lay shattered on the ground.

"Oh, no. It fell," George said.

"No," Terry said in a frighteningly calm voice. "It didn't fall. It was smashed. And I know exactly who did it."

In the center of the splintered glass lay a metal chain with two small rectangular metal plates attached. "They're dog tags," Nancy said in surprise. "The identification tags that soldiers wear." She leaned closer, and a chill went through her as she read the name on them. She looked up at Terry, who had gone completely white.

Terry carefully lifted the metal dog tags from the shattered glass. They dangled from his hand, a surprisingly bright silver. "I didn't think it was possible," he said softly. "But Nick Finney is back."

9

Dragon Latches

Nancy swiftly scanned the crowded display hall. "Nick Finney must still be nearby," she said. "You said he had a small, wiry build and bright red hair?"

"Don't even bother looking," Terry said, using a piece of cardboard to sweep up the broken glass. "Nick could melt in or out of sight like a shadow. He was being trained for intelligence work. Moving unseen was his specialty."

"Why did he smash the box, Dad?" Amy's voice shook.

"I don't know, pumpkin." Terry hugged Amy close to him. "I walked across the hall to talk to a friend. When I got back, the box was smashed."

"It's a warning," Nancy said.

Terry rubbed his chin. "That's what I think. And it's a warning I intend to take. Let's get packed up."

"But if Nick Finney is here, that means he's been

following you," Nancy said. "What's to stop him from following you home?"

"I'm guessing he's already on his way to Cherry Creek," Terry said. "Which is why we're going to the Peninsula."

"Oh, no," Amy said, backing away. "You're not leaving me with Aunt Marge again. She makes me eat boiled eggs for breakfast."

"Amy, don't start," her father said. "I'm taking you to the one place where I'll know you'll be safe."

Amy crossed her arms and turned her back on him.

"Fine, have a temper tantrum," Terry said. "It won't do you any good. I can't give you a choice this time." Without another word he began wrapping the stained-glass windows. Nancy, Bess, and George helped him pack up.

Reluctantly Amy followed them outside. "I just want you to know I think you're all acting like a bunch of cowards," she announced.

"Thank you for sharing that with us," Terry replied in a dry tone as they got into the van.

"And there's something none of you have thought of," Amy went on.

"What's that?" Nancy asked. Even if Amy was acting up, she was too sharp to ignore.

"Those dog tags don't mean that Nick Finney is back," Amy said. "What if someone else stole his dog tags and left them there?"

"The man in the dark red car," Bess said at once.

"I told you so," Amy said in a smug tone. "He's the one who was following us."

"That's even more reason to get you to the Peninsula," her father said between clenched teeth.

75

The ride south was a quiet one. Nancy wasn't sure if it was because everyone was thinking about Nick Finney and the man in the dark red car, or because there was a silent battle of wills going on between Terry and Amy.

The Peninsula was a good two and a half hours south of Cherry Creek. With a stop for lunch the ride from the show was about five hours altogether. It felt more like ten. Everyone except Amy seemed relieved when Terry finally pulled up in the driveway of a white split-level house.

"I don't like Aunt Marge's cooking," Amy said, eyeing the house with distaste.

"Amy, get out of the car," her father said, his patience clearly at an end.

Amy looked at Nancy. "Promise you'll call if anything exciting happens?"

"I promise," Nancy said.

The three friends watched the Kirklands walk up to the house, ring the doorbell, and be admitted by a boy who looked about Amy's age.

"Maybe we should ask to stay, too," Bess said in a worried tone. "I don't like the idea of going back to Cherry Creek and finding someone who was supposed to be dead waiting for us."

"Terry offered to help us find another place to stay," Nancy said. "We could take him up on that."

"No, we can't," George said. "Take a look at that." She pointed to the front door of the house, where Terry and his daughter had just emerged. Terry looked annoyed, and Amy looked triumphant. "I have a funny feeling we're still on call as baby-sitters."

"What happened?" Bess asked as both Kirklands got back into the van and Terry started it up.

"My sister's three-year-old has the chicken pox," he replied.

"And I've never had them," Amy added, sounding very pleased with herself. "Dad can't risk exposing me."

"No. Instead I'm going to expose you to someone who shot out my tire with a Colt .45, broke into the house three different times, nearly ran Nancy off the road, and now destroys my work in the middle of a crowded art show. I must be crazy."

"At least I won't get the chicken pox," Amy said.

"Maybe we should *all* take hotel rooms," George suggested.

"Putting up you three is no problem," Terry said at once. "I'll be glad to get rooms for you in the hotel of your choice. But how long are Amy and I supposed to avoid our own house? My studio is there. If I'm not home, I can't work."

"Amy could stay with us," Bess offered.

"I'm not leaving my dad!" Amy insisted.

"What about police protection?" George asked. "Can't you get them to watch the house?"

"I can barely get Detective Brower to return a phone call," Terry said bitterly. "I already asked for protection and was told there wasn't enough staff."

Nancy knew her own decision had been made, but she didn't want to endanger her friends. "I'm going back to Cherry Creek with Terry and Amy," she told Bess and George. "But there's a nice bed and breakfast inn the next town over. Maybe you should stay there for a couple of nights—until things calm down."

"No way," George said. "We're in this together."

"Right," Bess added loyally, but she didn't sound as sure.

Amy grinned at the three friends. "It sounds like we've still got a full house."

Terry shook his head as he drove toward the city. "Sounds like we're all crazy."

"Do you have the camera?" Nancy asked Joanne the next morning as they entered a café in Sausalito. They'd decided to have breakfast before going to the gallery. Joanne chose an outdoor table in the sun, then sat down and reached into her shirt pocket. She took something out and opened her palm, revealing a miniature camera. It couldn't have been more than three inches long.

"This took those great pictures?" Nancy asked doubtfully. "I mean, it's adorable and all—"

"But it looks like a toy," Joanne said, finishing Nancy's thought. "Trust me. It really works. It even has a silent shutter, so no one hears it snapping. I like to think of it as my spy camera."

"That's good," Nancy said, "because that's exactly what we need. I think there was something in the stolen trunk that wound up in Mai's gallery. But I don't know what it is, so I'd like to photograph as many of the things there as possible, even if we don't get into the back room. Photograph anything and everything that could have fit into a trunk that was two feet by three feet. And not just jade—ashtrays, files, anything."

"And you're going to distract Mr. Mai?"

"I'll do my best," Nancy said. "But I think once I get him started lecturing, he'll pretty much take care of that himself. Last time he got so wrapped up in what he was saying that he didn't pay much attention to me." She smiled. "Except when I raced out of his gallery to chase his nephew."

A waitress brought them blueberry muffins and juice. "So," Joanne said, sipping her juice, "you ask questions and I secretly take photographs. Then what?"

Nancy shrugged. "I guess we get the photographs developed and hope we got lucky."

At three minutes to ten Nancy and Joanne entered the Fe T'sui Gallery. "Omigosh," Joanne whispered, gazing at the jade collection. "I wonder if Keith's been here. If he hasn't, he'll flip when he sees it."

This time Nancy didn't have to be announced. At exactly ten o'clock Mr. Mai emerged from the back room. "Ms. Drew," he said with a curt nod. He stopped short as his gaze fell on Joanne. "You brought a companion?"

"This is Joanne Koslow, my cousin," Nancy said. "Joanne is the one who originally got me interested in Asian studies."

Joanne took her lead smoothly. "I stopped by Nancy's house this morning to return a book, and when she told me where she was going, I begged her to take me along. I hope you won't mind my showing up unannounced like this."

"You're also in Asian studies?" Mr. Mai asked.

Joanne flashed him a dazzling smile. "Actually, I'm specializing in antique silk kimonos."

79

Nancy winced inwardly, but Mr. Mai didn't seem put off. "Very well," he said. "Ms. Drew, you said you had a few more questions."

"Yes," Nancy said, taking out her notebook and moving toward a case filled with small statues. "How exactly were figures like this used? Would you find them in houses or only in temples?"

Half an hour later Nancy had run out of questions. Unfortunately, Mr. Mai wasn't nearly as talkative this morning as he'd been during their first interview. Nancy wondered if it was because she'd brought along a second person. She deliberately hadn't let herself look at Joanne. She didn't want to draw attention to what her friend was doing.

For her part Joanne had followed along, occasionally asking a question. To Nancy's surprise, Joanne sounded like someone who'd actually studied Asian art. She quoted dates and dynasties as easily as the gallery owner. Even Mr. Mai seemed to be impressed.

When they had reached the last of the display cases, there was a long, awkward silence. Nancy felt sure Mr. Mai was going to end the interview. How will I get a look at the back room? she wondered.

"Do you have any more questions, Ms. Drew?" asked Mr. Mai.

"Actually, yes," Nancy said, sounding nervous. "The other day when I, uh, chased your nephew through the back room, I lost a turquoise earring. Would it be possible for me to take a quick look and see if it's in there?"

"We found no earring," Mr. Mai replied.

"It's a very small earring," Nancy said. "It's hard to

see if you don't know you're supposed to be looking for it. Would you mind if I had a quick look?"

Mr. Mai checked his gold watch. "I have a client coming in five minutes. You understand that I'll have to ask you to leave when she arrives."

"I'll help you look," Joanne volunteered cheerfully. "After all, I gave you those earrings."

Mr. Mai led the way into the back room and stood watching as Nancy and Joanne began to search. The room was a combination office and shop. Shipping crates and cartons were stacked neatly along the back wall. Four broad worktables held jade figurines and the pedestals used to display them. One corner of the room was taken up by a desk and several tall file cabinets.

Nancy scanned the room, looking for anything that might provide a clue. Her eye was drawn to a pale green statue sitting on a display pedestal in the corner. The carving, made of a perfectly translucent piece of jade, was of a tiger. The tiger looked as if it were stalking. Nancy stared at the statue, unable to believe so much life had been captured in a piece of rock. She wouldn't have been at all surprised if the little jade tiger had roared and jumped off the pedestal. "What an incredible carving," she said in a hushed tone. "Why isn't it out front on display?"

"It just came in," Mr. Mai responded in a clipped tone. "Besides, it's not for sale. A private collector has already bid on it. Your earring, Ms. Drew?"

"Oh, right," Nancy said. She felt her face flush slightly. Nancy cast her eyes down to the floor,

81

searching for the earring that she knew was safe in Terry's house. And then she saw them. On the floor beneath the stand that displayed the jade tiger were two brass latches shaped like dragons.

Nancy blinked and looked again. They had to be the latches from Nick Finney's trunk.

10

Unsettling Questions

Nancy's eyes met Joanne's. *Please photograph the tiger and the brass latches beneath the workbench,* she pleaded silently. But she had no way of knowing whether or not Joanne would understand. She didn't even know if Joanne had used all the film in her camera.

Behind Nancy, Mr. Mai coughed impatiently. "Ms. Drew," he began, "I'm sorry, but I really must ask you to leave now."

Nancy pretended to be disappointed. "I don't see my earring anywhere. What about you, Joanne?"

Joanne shook her head, looking similarly disappointed. Then she and Nancy thanked Mr. Mai for his time and left the gallery.

Nancy waited until they were safely in her car before she spoke. "Did you see them?" she asked. "In the back room, on the floor beneath the tiger statue— the latches from Nick Finney's trunk."

"Seen and photographed," Joanne said. "Now all we have to do is develop the photos and bring them to the police. Then they'll know Mr. Mai had the trunk."

"Let's hope so," Nancy said. "Terry called the police station early this morning to see what information their lab had gotten on the pieces of the trunk I found behind the gallery. They said the only prints on it were Terry's, Amy's, and mine. They also told him that finding pieces of the trunk behind the gallery wasn't enough to question Mr. Mai, who's a very well-respected art dealer."

Joanne patted her tiny camera. "Well, I took shots of everything I could."

"Thank goodness Mr. Mai didn't notice he had a photographer walking around his gallery," Nancy said. "Of course, you made a very convincing student. Where did you learn all those facts you were rattling off?"

"Hang around Keith long enough and you just absorb them. I always thought it was neat stuff but never thought I'd actually use it." Joanne grinned. "I guess I'm sort of an honorary Asian art student."

Nancy smiled at her friend. "You know something? For an honorary Asian art student, you make a pretty good detective."

Nancy dropped Joanne at her car, and the two girls split up. Nancy had arranged to go back to Terry's house to pick up Bess and George. Then the three friends would drive to Joanne's for the last of the wedding projects: baking the cake.

George was on one of the outside decks when Nancy reached Terry's house. Wearing faded red sweats and a headband, she arched backward with her palms flat on the deck, fingertips nearly touching her feet.

"Why are you stretching out?" Nancy asked.

"This may be the only real exercise I get this week," George replied, coming upright by doing a perfect walkover.

"Where's Bess?" Nancy asked.

"Upstairs. Amy's at school, and Terry's in his studio." George stretched to the side and gave Nancy a quizzical look. "Have you given any thought to what we're about to do?"

Nancy chuckled. "You mean baking a cake for three hundred people?"

Bess opened the screen door to the deck and walked outside. She was wearing a short aqua skirt and a white blouse. "We'd better get going," Bess said. "I wonder if Joanne will let us sample some of the cake after we bake it," she added as she and her friends headed for the car.

"You mean, just to make sure it tastes okay for the guests?" George said with a laugh.

"Yeah," Bess replied. "Just to make sure."

The girls drove to Joanne's discussing what kind of cake they would each have if they were getting married.

When they arrived in Joanne's kitchen, she handed Nancy a five-pound bag of shelled walnuts. "You can start by chopping these. I'd let you use the food processor, but I need to stir the batter."

"That's all right," Nancy said. She looked at the chopping board and knife and felt a bit dazed. She couldn't quite believe that the four of them were actually going to bake a chocolate-carrot cake that would look like a castle and feed three hundred people. But Joanne and Bess both seemed sure it would work, and neither Nancy nor George was about to argue.

Nancy began to chop walnuts, enjoying the coziness of Joanne's cheerful kitchen. To her surprise, it felt good to be away from the case for a while. The four friends talked about growing up together in River Heights, and how the small midwestern city was still very much the same as it had been when Joanne left.

At last the talk turned back to the present. Nancy and Joanne told George and Bess what had gone on that morning at the gallery.

"So when do we get to see those photographs?" George asked.

"Soon," Joanne promised. "I took them to the print shop this morning. Keith is going to pick them up on his way here from his last class."

"Did you tell Terry about the brass latches?" Bess asked Nancy.

Nancy finished chopping the last of the walnuts. "Not yet. I wanted to have the photographs first."

A short time later, the doorbell rang, and Keith came in, carrying a tan envelope. He bowed to Joanne with a flourish. "As you requested, my lady. What are these, anyway, that you needed them so quickly?"

"I'll show you," Joanne replied. "Photo break, everyone," she announced to her friends. "Let's go into the living room and see what we've got."

Joanne handed Nancy the envelope. Trying to control her eagerness, Nancy looked through the prints one by one. Joanne had followed her directions exactly. At first there were pictures of everyday objects that might have fit inside the trunk: a clock, a book, a pad, a stapler, and other assorted items.

"Great ash tray," Keith teased. "And a very exciting photograph."

"Patience," Joanne said. "The best is yet to come."

Next came the gallery's exhibit. Nancy was amazed at how many of the carvings Joanne had been able to photograph and how clearly they came out in spite of reflections from the display cases.

"That's an eighteenth-century Japanese piece," Keith said, identifying a dark green jade pendant. "And this amulet is probably from China at the turn of the century."

"There!" Nancy exclaimed as she found the photograph of the brass dragon latches. "I think we've got our proof that Mr. Mai had Terry's trunk."

"I'm still confused," Bess said. "Does that mean someone stole the trunk and sold it to Mr. Mai? Or did Mr. Mai have someone steal it for him?"

"And we're still not sure if there was anything in the hidden compartment," George pointed out. "What if Mai opened it and there was nothing inside?"

"I don't have the answers to any of those questions yet," Nancy admitted, "but I will."

"Wow!" The soft exclamation came from Keith. "I've never seen anything this fine before—except in museums."

Nancy glanced over to see what he was looking at. It was a photograph of the jade tiger. "That's the one I loved, too," she told Keith. "Mr. Mai didn't even have it on display out front—it was in the back room. He said it just came in, and it's already been bid on by a private collector." She looked at Keith curiously. "How old do you think it is?"

Keith studied the photograph for a moment before answering. "It's hard to tell without seeing the thing up close, but I'd guess it's not that old, as jade goes. I'd say it was carved sometime during the eighteen hundreds. It's the type of statue you'd find in Buddhist temples built during that period." He held the photo up to the window and examined it again. "I could be wrong, but this looks like Burmese jade, which, as everyone in Asia will tell you, is the finest jade in the world. And whoever did the carving was incredibly talented. This piece may be worth as much as everything else in the gallery combined."

"I knew you had good taste," Bess said to Nancy.

"Speaking of taste," Joanne broke in, "we've got a lot of cake to bake. The wedding is only three days away, which means the photo break is officially over."

Keith joined the kitchen crew, and they began pouring batter into sheet-cake pans. The delicious smell of chocolate-carrot cake filled the kitchen as the five friends cleaned up. It was just after sunset when the last dish was washed and the last cake came out of the oven and was set on a rack to cool.

"Today, cake. Tomorrow, icing and assembly," said Joanne with a sigh of satisfaction. At the look of alarm on her friends' faces, she quickly added, "Don't worry, I can handle that on my own."

"What's this?" Terry asked later that night when Nancy handed him the packet of photographs.

"Joanne and I went back to the Fe T'sui Gallery," she explained. "And Joanne took some pictures."

Terry and Amy had been watching TV. He turned down the sound, balancing the envelope in his hand as if trying to sense what was inside. "Did Mr. Mai know you were photographing his gallery?"

"I don't think so. Joanne's camera is only a couple of inches big, and she was careful."

"I hope so," Terry said.

"I think we found the brass latches from Nick's trunk," Nancy told him. "I need you to look at these."

"I want to see them, too," Amy said. She was perched on the arm of her father's chair.

Terry opened the envelope and slowly began going through the prints.

"Can't you go a little faster?" Amy asked impatiently. "I want to see the dragon latches."

"Hush," Terry murmured. He stopped at the picture of the jade tiger. "Nice carving," he said, then examined it more closely. "This looks like stuff we used to see in Vietnam. I remember we passed one temple that was completely outdoors. The monks had statues like this set in a rock wall."

"Dad," Amy said, "let's get to the important picture, okay?"

"Maybe you ought to go to bed," Terry suggested.

"Never mind," Amy said quickly.

Nancy listened to this exchange with one ear. Ever since the art show yesterday, Amy had been unusually edgy. Had Nick Finney's reappearance upset her?

"Finally!" Amy exclaimed as her father flipped to the photograph of the two brass latches.

"They're the latches from Nick's trunk, all right," Terry agreed.

"Then the case is solved," Amy declared. "All we have to do is show this to Detective Brower."

"I'm not sure that's a good idea," said her father, looking at Nancy with concern. "If you didn't have Mr. Mai's permission to take these pictures, he might be able to press charges against you. You were in his gallery under false pretenses. And the police aren't crazy about civilians spying on each other."

"Reporters do it all the time," George argued.

"If Nancy or Joanne had a press pass, it would be a different story," Terry said. "And perhaps if we were working with a more cooperative police department, things would be different. All I'm saying is I'm not sure you want to go to the police with this."

"What are we supposed to do?" Amy demanded indignantly. "Drop the case?"

Terry didn't seem to hear her. "I'd give a lot to know what was in that trunk," he mused. "Something that wound up in Mai's gallery."

Nancy reached for the photo of the jade tiger. "You said you saw things like this in Vietnam?"

He nodded.

"The brass latches were lying on the floor underneath a pedestal," Nancy said. "The jade tiger was sitting on top of that same pedestal."

"Does that mean the tiger was hidden in Nick Finney's trunk?" Amy asked.

"Maybe," Nancy said. "We don't know for sure."

Terry shook his head. "If it is true, I can't help thinking about how Nick got the statue. I don't know

90

anything about jade, but even I can see this thing is worth a fortune. Nick didn't have any money. And it's not the sort of thing someone gives as a present."

"Maybe he didn't know the jade tiger was in there," Bess suggested. "Maybe he just thought he was asking you to hold a trunk for him."

Terry leaned his head back against the chair and shut his eyes. "That's what I want to believe, Bess. And before yesterday I would have. But after that little incident at the art show, I think we have to consider another possibility." He opened his eyes and looked at Nancy, who knew exactly what he meant.

"You think Nick stole the jade tiger from a temple back in Vietnam," she said.

"Bingo." Terry glanced at his watch, got up, and turned the sound up on the TV. "Sorry," he said, "but I've got a show in Mendocino tomorrow, and I need to hear a weather report. They've been predicting rain and fog for a few days now."

The local newscast was on, but the newscasters hadn't gotten to the weather.

"Good grief! Is that what I think it is?" George asked as a photograph of the jade tiger appeared on the TV screen.

The news anchor's voice confirmed it. "The Fe T'sui Gallery in Sausalito was robbed this evening. A statue of a jade tiger was taken. It is estimated to be worth over seventy thousand dollars."

"I'm going to bed," Amy announced.

Her father looked at her in surprise. "Of your own free will?"

Amy wrinkled her nose at him, said good night, and headed upstairs.

"Wonders never cease," Terry murmured, and it occurred to Nancy that he was right. Why had Amy been so interested in the trunk and then gone to bed so suddenly? She'd figure it out later, she decided. Right now, something else was becoming clear.

"See if this makes sense," she said to her friends. "Let's say the tiger was hidden in Nick's trunk. Someone broke in here and stole it. Somehow the tiger and the trunk wound up in Mr. Mai's gallery. And now it's been stolen a second time."

George grinned. "And the suspects are—"

"The man in the dark red car and Mr. Mai's nephew, Jimmy. Maybe Mr. Mai, too. He could have put someone else up to it. And we also have a phantom suspect, Nick Finney. I think," Nancy said slowly, "that all along there's been more than one person after that statue."

"You're probably right," George agreed. "Now all we have to do is figure out who they are."

"What I don't understand," Terry said, "is why they haven't left us alone. The trunk was taken from the house days ago. You'd think that at that point whoever was after the tiger had what they wanted. The danger should be over."

"But it's not," Bess said with a chill.

"No," Nancy said, "it's not."

Terry had already left for Mendocino, and Amy for school the next morning, when the doorbell rang.

"I'll get it," Nancy said to George and Bess, who were still finishing their breakfasts.

She opened the front door to find Detective Brower and a uniformed officer standing outside. "Ms. Drew," Detective Brower said, "I'm afraid I have to ask you to come with us. You're wanted for questioning in the theft of a jade tiger."

11

Kidnapped!

Nancy stood in the Kirklands' hallway, staring at the detective in disbelief.

"Wait a minute," said George, who had followed Nancy to the door. "Are you saying that Nancy is under arrest?"

"Not under arrest, no," Detective Brower replied. "At least, not right now. But I'll need Ms. Drew to come to the police station for questioning."

"I'm going with you," George told Nancy.

"And me," added Bess, who'd joined them.

Detective Brower frowned at them. "You two will have to follow in your own vehicle," he said brusquely. "Now, Ms. Drew, please come with us."

Nancy got her jacket, wondering why the police wanted her for questioning. She knew she had nothing to do with the theft of the jade tiger. But what if Mr. Mai had somehow discovered that she and Joanne had secretly photographed his gallery? Was Joanne going to be brought in as well?

The ride to the station was short. Neither Detective Brower nor the uniformed officer spoke. Once inside the station Nancy was led to a small, windowless room. Detective Brower and the uniformed officer followed her inside. There was nothing in the room except a bare table and three chairs. Nancy and the two policemen sat down.

"Ms. Drew," the detective began, "we're going to ask you a few questions. You've heard that a very valuable jade statue was stolen from the Fe T'sui Gallery in Sausalito?"

"I saw it on the news last night," Nancy answered calmly.

"But you saw the tiger itself yesterday morning."

"Mr. Mai gave me a tour of his gallery," Nancy replied, wondering exactly what Mr. Mai had told the police. If Mai had told them she was an art student and they found out she was lying, she'd definitely seem suspicious. Nancy wished her father were around. She had an awful feeling that she was going to need a lawyer.

"Mr. Mai said that was the second time you were in the gallery," the detective went on. "The first time his talk with you ended when you suddenly sprinted through his back room. The second time you brought a friend and made an excuse to go into the back room. He said you were very taken with the tiger."

For the hundredth time Nancy wished that Detective Brower were like most of the police she'd worked with. Then she could just explain that she was working on the case, conducting her own investigation. She could even tell Brower what she'd discovered so far. But she knew that if she tried to explain things to this man, it would only make matters worse than they already were.

"Detective Brower," she said, "am I a suspect in the robbery?"

"You may be," he replied. "You did, after all, show a definite interest in the stolen object."

"Do you think I'd call attention to the statue if I wanted to steal it?" Nancy asked incredulously. "Why would I be that obvious? I couldn't help noticing that carving. It was the most beautiful thing in the gallery. Anyone would notice it."

Detective Brower did not look convinced.

"If I'm a suspect," Nancy said, "then I want to talk to a lawyer."

No sooner had she said this than there was a knock on the door, and a young woman wearing a pale gray suit stepped in. Detective Brower looked distinctly annoyed. "Sayers," he growled, "what are you doing here?"

The young woman held out her hand to Nancy. "I'm Alison Sayers, an attorney. I just had a call from your father—he asked me to represent you."

"How did he know?" Nancy asked in amazement.

"Never mind that," Brower snapped.

"I'd like a few minutes alone with my client," Alison Sayers told the police in a firm voice.

"And I know exactly what will happen next," Detective Brower said. "Every time we ask a question, she's going to take the fifth and refuse to answer."

Alison Sayers smiled. "You don't have any evidence against her, do you?"

"Not yet," Brower answered. He sighed deeply, then he and the uniformed officer left the room. Nancy quickly filled Ms. Sayers in on what had happened.

"Well," the lawyer said, "what we have to tell the police is that you didn't steal the tiger or have anything to do with its theft. You won't have to answer too many other questions right now."

Nancy did exactly as Ms. Sayers advised, which didn't make Detective Brower very happy. At last he said, "Let's not waste any more time, Ms. Drew. You're free to go on the condition that you remain in this area until you hear from us."

"Fine," Nancy said with relief.

She and Ms. Sayers walked out of the interview room to find Bess and George waiting anxiously. "Aha," Nancy said. "I know how my father found out about this."

"We called him from Terry's house," Bess explained. "The minute you left with Brower."

"And he must have called me the minute he got off the phone with you," Ms. Sayers added.

"Thank goodness," Nancy said.

"It's not over yet," the lawyer said in a worried tone. "Detective Brower isn't going to drop this until the jade tiger is found."

"No," Nancy agreed. "It isn't enough that we have to watch out for the blond-haired man, Mr. Mai's nephew, and the ghost of Nick Finney. Now we also have to watch out for the police."

* * *

"Is it really possible?" George asked. She was sitting on her bed in the room the three friends shared, writing a postcard to her family. "We actually have a day with no wedding chores and no detective work?"

"If you don't count rescuing me from the police this morning," Nancy said. "Personally, I think it's a good idea to lay low for a while. I don't want Detective Brower getting too interested in us."

"I'm all for that," Bess said. "Besides, this means we can go to the Calistoga mud baths. Imagine, sinking down into a tub of warm, energizing mud."

"Are you sure you don't want to rent mountain bikes?" George asked hopefully. "Remember, you wanted to lose five pounds."

"Let's toss a coin," Nancy suggested. "Heads we take mud baths, tails we rent bikes. Either way, we have to be back by three to pick up Amy from school."

Nancy tossed the coin, and George won. George found a nearby rental shop in the phone book. The three friends changed into biking gear. Nancy put on navy leggings and a white sweatshirt. George wore cutoffs and a T-shirt under her blue windbreaker. Both were surprised to see that Bess wore a pair of tight black cycling shorts and a light green cycling jersey.

"I didn't know you bicycled," Nancy said.

"I don't," Bess assured her cheerfully. "I just believe in having clothes for every occasion."

After they packed water bottles and a light lunch, Nancy and her friends set off for the rental shop. The owner, a young woman with long, honey-colored hair, supplied the three girls with ten-speed mountain bikes that had sturdy frames and wide wheels. "You're in a prime area for cycling," she said. "There are dozens of off-road trails all over Marin. They aren't open to cars, and they're perfect for bicycles." She pointed to a trail map on the wall behind her. "What level of difficulty do you want? Intermediate?"

"Intermediate beginner," Bess said quickly.

The woman laughed. "I think I know the perfect trail." She pointed to a squiggly line on Mount Tamalpais. "The loop around Lake Lagunitas is one of the prettiest rides on the mountain. And there's only one real hill, which you can walk if you want."

"Sounds perfect," Bess said.

The girls soon found that the woman's advice had been excellent. The trail circled the shores of the deep blue lake. Except for a few places where they had to either splash through streams or ride along narrow, wooden bridges, the ride was an easy one. After a while they sat down to eat a late lunch beneath a grand old oak tree.

"That was fun," Bess said as they returned the bikes. "Do you think I lost my five pounds?"

Nancy and George looked at each other, but neither answered. Instead, George asked what time it was.

Nancy looked at her watch. "I can't believe it," she said with a groan. "It's already ten of three. Amy gets out of school in ten minutes, and it will take us at least twenty to get there."

"Don't worry," George said. "She knows we're going to pick her up. She'll wait."

By the time Nancy and her friends arrived at Amy's

school, it was three-fifteen. "Why did we have to get stuck in a traffic jam today?" Nancy moaned as she parked in front of the low brick building. Children were still trickling out of the main door. Some headed for a nearby school bus. Others got into waiting cars. Groups of two and three walked home together.

Almost ten minutes later it looked as if the last of the children had left the building.

"This doesn't feel right," Nancy said, frowning slightly. "Amy should have been out by now."

"Maybe she didn't see us," Bess said.

"We've been sitting right in front of the school, and she'd recognize her father's car," George pointed out. "She must have figured we weren't coming when we were late. I guess she left before we arrived."

Nancy got out of the car. "Maybe she's still inside, talking to a teacher or a friend. I'm going to find out."

As Nancy entered the school building her feeling of unease deepened. The halls were silent. She walked past empty classrooms. There was no one in sight, and her footsteps echoed loudly.

She felt a little better when she saw lights on in the school office at the end of the hall. She found a woman standing in front of a copy machine.

"Excuse me," Nancy said, entering the office. "I'm here to pick up Amy Kirkland. Do you know where she is?"

"Amy . . . she's a fourth-grader, right?"

"That's right."

"Let me try her classroom and see if her teacher is still in," the woman said, then made a brief phone call.

A few minutes later a middle-aged woman wearing

a tan dress walked in. "I'm Mrs. Shields," she said. "Amy's teacher."

"My name is Nancy Drew. I'm a friend of the Kirkland family. I was supposed to pick up Amy at three, but I arrived late, and there's no sign of her now. Did you see her leave the building?"

"Our class ended late today," the teacher replied. "I saw Amy wait for a bit and then start walking. Sometimes Amy's father picks her up, and sometimes she goes home on her own. They don't live that far from the school, so it didn't seem unusual."

"Except that Amy was supposed to wait for me today," Nancy said.

"She did wait for a while," Mrs. Shields reminded her gently. "Perhaps she thought she missed you." The teacher looked at her watch. "If Amy walked home, she ought to be there by now. Why don't you call the house?"

Nancy made the call even though she was sure no one would be home. There was no answer.

A line of tension appeared across Mrs. Shields's forehead. "I have another idea. Amy's friend Patricia lives down the road from the Kirklands'. Patricia's been out sick for the last few days. Maybe Amy stopped to visit her."

Mrs. Shields dialed Patricia's number and handed the phone to Nancy. Patricia's mother picked up the phone. "No," she said, "Amy isn't here. But it's strange that you're asking about her. I just saw her a few minutes ago."

"You did?" Nancy asked.

"I went to get a prescription for Patricia. I was driving home from the pharmacist's when I saw Amy on Widmer Road." Nancy knew Widmer was the road below the one that led onto Terry's drive. "She was with someone."

"Who?" Nancy asked, dreading the answer.

"A big blond-haired man. She got into his car, a red one." The woman's voice faltered. "Now that I think about it, it was quite odd. But I've been so worried about Patricia's running a fever, I'm afraid I didn't pay much attention to Amy. I hope she's all right."

"Thank you," Nancy said, hanging up. She had an aching, hollow feeling in her stomach. It felt as if someone had just knocked the wind out of her.

"What is it?" Mrs. Shields asked. "You don't look very well."

"The news isn't good," Nancy replied in a shaky voice. "Amy Kirkland's been kidnapped."

12

A Warning from the Past

Nancy stood in the school office, feeling paralyzed by what she'd just heard. The man in the dark red car had kidnapped Amy. She couldn't let herself think about what might happen to the girl. Instead, she forced herself to remain calm. The important thing now was to find a way to help Amy before it was too late.

"We'd better call the police," she told Mrs. Shields.

"What about Amy's father?" the teacher asked.

The Mendocino art show was a two-day exhibit, and Terry had not planned to return home until the next afternoon.

"I have the number of his hotel," Nancy said. "I'll call there next."

Nancy called the police and was relieved when she learned that Detective Brower was out. Instead, Officer Grant asked Nancy and Mrs. Shields to remain at the school until a squad car arrived. The police would need them both to file the report.

Next she called Terry's hotel. He wasn't in, but she left a message for him to call her at the house as soon as possible. She just couldn't leave a message saying his daughter had been kidnapped.

"My friends Bess and George are waiting for me," Nancy told Mrs. Shields when she hung up. "I'd better tell them what happened."

Nancy returned to the car. Bess and George were standing outside, leaning against the hood.

"Where's Amy?" Bess asked as Nancy approached.

"Oh, no," George said after taking one look at Nancy's face. "Don't tell me . . ."

"Amy's been kidnapped by the man in the dark red car," Nancy said shakily. "We have to wait here until the police come." She shut her eyes briefly. "How are we ever going to explain this to Terry?"

Nearly two hours later the three friends returned to the empty Kirkland house. "It feels awful coming back here without Amy," Bess said.

"I know," Nancy said. She hung up her jacket and tried once again to reach Terry.

"I'm sorry," said the hotel desk clerk. "Mr. Kirkland still hasn't returned."

"When he does, would you please have him call his home?" Nancy asked. "Tell him it's urgent!"

"Of course," the man replied.

"No luck?" George guessed as she hung up.

"Actually, I'm kind of relieved he wasn't there," Nancy admitted to her friends. "I don't know how I can tell him that his daughter's been kidnapped. I feel

104

so awful that we were late. I'm hoping the police will have some good news before he calls back."

"What I don't understand," Bess said, "is why Amy would have gone off with a stranger."

"I've been wondering about that, too," Nancy said. "The only thing I can think of is that he threatened her."

George paced restlessly. "If only we knew more about the blond-haired man."

"I know he's dangerous," Nancy said with a shudder. "I can't stand to think that Amy is his captive."

"There's got to be something we can do," Bess said.

Nancy sighed in defeat. "If there is I don't know what it is. I think all we can do now is wait."

"I hate waiting," George complained.

"Then help me make dinner," Bess said, trying to keep busy.

The two cousins made pasta for dinner. Although everyone made an effort to eat, no one had an appetite. Later, the girls cleaned up the kitchen, rubbing at the counters long after they'd come clean.

"Why don't we put on the news?" George suggested as they stood in the spotless kitchen. "I don't really think they'd mention Amy this soon, but you never know."

They settled down in front of the television. Again Nancy found her thoughts drifting. Where was Amy now? Who was the man in the dark red car and what did he really want? Was Amy's kidnapping connected to the theft of the jade tiger?

"Oh, look!" Bess cried out as the photograph of the jade tiger appeared on the TV screen.

But the news announcer only reported that no progress had been made on the case.

"No kidding," Nancy agreed. She was sure that the tiger and the blond-haired man were connected somehow, but she was still missing a vital piece of information.

The evening passed slowly. The girls tried unsuccessfully to watch TV, play Monopoly, and do a crossword puzzle, but their thoughts always drifted back to Amy.

"This is ridiculous," George said at last. "Let's stop pretending to keep busy. We might as well just be honest and sit and worry."

The phone rang then. Nancy ran to get it, praying that it was the police with good news. Instead, she heard Terry's voice. "I already know what happened," he said in an amazingly calm tone. "The police found me about five minutes ago. I'm leaving Mendocino now. I'll be there as soon as I can."

By midnight both Bess and George were asleep in the living room, each one tucked under a blanket. Terry had come home about an hour earlier. After checking with the police and finding there was still no word, he'd vanished into his studio. Nancy sat alone in the quiet house. Although her eyes were getting heavy, she knew she coudln't sleep, not until she knew something more about Amy.

She started as she heard a sound near the front of the house. It's just trees brushing against the windows, she told herself. No, it was definitely someone approaching the house. Nancy peered out the window. There were no lights, nothing she could see. Chills ran through her. Was the intruder back?

She turned toward the studio to alert Terry. Then the front door opened and a white-faced Amy walked in.

"Amy!" Nancy cried.

"What?" Bess mumbled, sitting up.

Terry was there at once, gathering his daughter in his arms. "Are you all right?" he asked in a husky voice.

Amy clung to her father, sobbing hysterically.

"Could one of you call the pediatrician?" Terry asked over his daughter's head. "Her number's by the phone in the kitchen. Ask if she can come right away. Tell her it's an emergency. And then call the police and tell them Amy's home."

George went to make the calls.

Amy lifted her tear-streaked face from her father's shoulder. "I'm okay," she said, her voice trembling. "I wasn't hurt. I was just scared."

"What happened?" Terry asked. His voice was equally shaky. "Why did you go with the man in the dark red car?"

George came back into the room and reported that the doctor was on her way.

Amy looked up at her father. "I want to go to bed now. Okay?"

"In a little while, pumpkin. I want the doctor to look at you first. Now tell us what happened."

The girl stared at the floor and shook her head.

"I'm not going to be angry with you," Terry said gently. "But we have to get as much information as we can so we can find this man. So he never does anything like this again. I need you to tell me what happened."

"I can't," Amy said, her entire body trembling.

"Why not?" Nancy asked. She knew that the girl was on the verge of breaking down again.

Amy spoke directly to her father. "He told me that if I told anyone, he would take you out. That means kill you."

"I know what it means," Terry said grimly.

Amy folded her arms across her chest. "I'm not going to say anything else. Not to you or the police."

Her father tried one last time. "Amy, the man who kidnapped you is evil. We can't do what he wants us to do. We've got to stop him. That means you have to tell us everything you can."

The doorbell rang then, and Amy's doctor came in. She immediately took Amy upstairs to examine her. The police arrived a few moments later. Everyone waited downstairs until the doctor announced that Amy was unharmed but desperately in need of a good night's sleep.

"I'm afraid I'll need to talk to her first," Officer Grant said.

The doctor nodded. "All right, but only for a few minutes. She's still very upset."

Nancy and Terry went upstairs with the police officer. But although Officer Grant did everything he could to persuade Amy to talk, the girl refused to say any more. She turned away from them, her face buried in her pillow.

Terry looked helplessly at the police officer. "I'd like her to get some sleep. What if we try again in the morning?"

Officer Grant scratched his head. "All right, let her sleep," he agreed. "We'll talk tomorrow."

Terry stayed with his daughter until she fell asleep. Nancy went downstairs with the police officer. "Did you talk to Patricia's mother?" she asked.

"We certainly did, but she didn't tell us much more than she told you." He gave Nancy a sharp look. "This is the third report we've had on that man. You saw his car coming down the drive after Kirkland's tire was shot out. Then, according to Officer Harlan, he tried to run you off the road. Now he kidnaps the little girl."

Nancy nodded.

Officer Grant put on his hat and went to the door. "Sounds to me as if he's trying to warn someone away from something. Maybe it's Kirkland he's trying to warn. And maybe it's you."

Nancy swallowed hard. "I'll be careful," she said as she shut the door. She was in complete agreement with the officer. The fair-haired man was sending out warnings. But what was it he was warning them away from?

She started as Terry entered the room. "Amy's asleep," he said. He rubbed his eyes and went to stand by one of the living room windows. "Quite a night, huh?"

"More excitement than even I like," Nancy admitted. "I'm so glad Amy's safe. She's a brave girl, and she's totally determined to protect you."

"I wish I was doing a better job of protecting her," Terry said. He held out a folded slip of paper. "I found this in the pocket of Amy's jacket."

Nancy unfolded the paper. Printed in block letters

was a message that read, "Kirkland, get rid of Nancy Drew, or next time Amy takes a ride with Mr. D."

There were two initials scrawled below the message in a script that Nancy couldn't decipher. "Mr. D?" she asked. "Do you know a Mr. D?"

"Oh, I know Mr. D, all right," Terry said with a soft, mirthless laugh. "I met him for the first time in Vietnam. All the soldiers used to talk about him as if he were a companion. And he was, you know. We were in the middle of a war. Mr. D seemed to be everywhere we turned." Terry's eyes were filled with pain. "Mr. D was our nickname for death."

13

A Hidden Threat

Nancy examined the note in her hand and knew what she had to tell Terry. "I'll drop the case," she said. "Nothing's worth putting Amy at that kind of risk."

"You know," Terry said, almost as if he hadn't heard her, "I keep thinking that crazy war is over. And every time I do, something new surfaces."

"Tomorrow Bess and George and I will move to a bed and breakfast," Nancy went on. "Maybe then this guy will be satisfied and leave you alone."

"That's not necessary," Terry said absently.

Nancy looked at the note again. Her mind was made up. She, Bess, and George would move out tomorrow. She'd give up the case. Still, she had to ask. "Terry, can you make out these initials?"

He glanced at the note. "N.F." he read.

"N.F.?" Nancy felt the excitement over a new clue race through her. "Those are Nick's initials!"

"That's right." Terry didn't sound nearly as excited as she did.

"Don't you see?" Nancy said. "Nick may not match the description of the man in the red car, but if he wrote the note, then maybe he's working with him."

"Nick didn't write that note."

"How can you be so sure?" Nancy asked.

"Because Nick was the one guy over there who never used the term Mr. D. He always talked about death as the Pilot." Terry shrugged. "I don't know why.

"Nick isn't the kidnapper," he went on. "Someone wanted me to think he was, and they made a mistake." He glanced at her and smiled. "I'm glad, if you want to know the truth. Nick and I were friends. I mean, could you imagine having a kid of your own and then having Bess kidnap her?"

Nancy smiled at the idea. "Not exactly, but Bess has never been the kidnapping type."

"Neither was Nick—at least, I didn't think so then."

"So that means someone else has been sabotaging you," Nancy said softly.

"Someone else who was in Vietnam," Terry finished the thought.

"And someone who wants to frame Nick," Nancy added.

"The problem is, that doesn't narrow things down much. There were a lot of us." He turned from the window. "Let me sleep on this. In the meantime"— he nodded toward the note—"let's just say I'm tired of being threatened. The three of you are welcome to stay as long as you like."

112

That night, as Nancy lay in bed, her eyes were drawn to the full moon shining through the stained-glass window. Forget-me-nots, she thought drowsily. The name of the flower played in her mind, as if it were a message. Her mind flashed on an image of the smashed glasswork and Nick Finney's dog tags. Maybe Nick didn't have anything to do with the kidnapping. But she couldn't help wondering if he was still alive.

"But I want to go to the park," Amy was saying as Nancy entered the kitchen the next morning. "I feel totally fine," she told her father. "Honest."

"Well, I'm glad," Terry said, "but that doesn't change the fact that Detective Brower called half an hour ago and asked me to bring you by the station."

"It won't do any good," Amy said quietly. "I'm not going to tell him anything."

Terry rinsed out his coffee mug. "If you won't tell us what happened, you're doing exactly what that man wants you to do. Don't you see that you're helping him?"

Amy folded her arms across her chest and stared out the window.

"Good morning," Nancy said.

"Morning," Terry replied, giving her a thoughtful glance. "All right," he said to Amy. "If you won't talk to me or the police, what about talking to Nancy?"

"I can't," Amy said.

Nancy put a slice of bread in the toaster. "Even if we keep it just between the two of us?"

Amy got up, turned her back on them, and headed out of the kitchen.

"Amy!" Terry's voice was unusually sharp.

She stopped at the door. "I'm sorry if I was rude," she said reluctantly. "Dad, can I go to the park *after* we see Detective Brower? Please? I'm supposed to meet Jimmy there."

"We'll talk about it later," her father answered. "Now get ready to go." He turned to Nancy with a sigh. "I apologize for my daughter's behavior. I think she's still upset about last night."

"I would be, too, if I'd been kidnapped," Nancy assured him. Her mind went back to the last thing Amy had said. "Do you know who Jimmy is?"

"Jimmy," Terry repeated. "I think he's in her class." He grinned. "He's the boy whose art projects all turn out looking like race cars."

Nancy listened to this, remembering Amy's wide-eyed expression when she'd first described Jimmy Thieu. It was time she had a talk with the girl.

Amy opened the door before Nancy even knocked. "What do you want?" she asked.

"I promise I won't ask you about the kidnapping," Nancy began, "but I'd like to talk to you."

Amy nodded, and Nancy followed her into the room. She noted that Amy's windows were the most beautiful of all. Each pane was framed by delicate purple morning glories winding through dark green vines.

"What a great room," Nancy said. The girl was silent, and Nancy turned to face her. "Amy, are you angry with me?"

Amy sighed and sat cross-legged on her bed. "I don't want my father hurt."

"I don't want anyone hurt, either," Nancy told her.

"Which is why I need to ask you about something else. Is the Jimmy you're meeting in the park today in your class?"

"Mr. Indy Five Hundred?" Amy asked with a grin. "No way. I'm going to see Jimmy Thieu. He's—" Her eyes widened and her grin vanished.

"Mr. Mai's nephew," Nancy finished.

Amy was silent again.

"He's your friend, isn't he?" Nancy asked.

"I practice speaking Vietnamese with him," Amy said at last. "My mother taught me. Then she died, and I didn't know anyone else who spoke it. Anyway, one Sunday I went to Sausalito with my friend Patricia and her parents. They have a boat there, and we went sailing. After, Patricia and I were hanging out on the dock, waiting for her parents to finish tying up the boat. This boy came up and began speaking Vietnamese. He asked me what I was doing so far from home."

Nancy looked at her questioningly.

"He meant Vietnam," Amy said. "He thought I was born there, too. I told him I wasn't, and we talked a little." Amy pushed back a lock of glossy black hair. "It felt great to speak Vietnamese again. I missed it."

Nancy listened silently.

"So once a month he rides up here on his dirt bike, and we just talk together," Amy finished. "He tells me what Vietnam was like. He wants to go back there someday."

"Is that what he was doing the night I met him in your driveway?" Nancy asked. "Coming to talk to you?"

Amy shook her head. "I don't know. I don't know why he was here."

115

"Did he know about the break-ins?" Nancy asked.

"Well, Jimmy did know I had the trunk. He was the one person I'd shown it to, because it was from Vietnam." Amy paused for a moment. "He knows everything that goes on in his uncle's gallery, too. He must have seen the trunk there and recognized it."

Nancy sat down on the girl's bed, trying to put all she'd heard together. "How do you know Jimmy isn't working with whoever broke into the house?"

"Because he'd never do that to me!" Amy insisted.

"All right," Nancy said in a soothing tone. "Jimmy wouldn't steal from you. He's your friend. Then why doesn't your father know about him?"

"Jimmy doesn't trust grown-ups, any of them. When he started coming up here, he made me promise not to tell any grown-ups about him." Amy gave Nancy a half smile. "You're only eighteen, so I guess you're still okay."

Nancy thought back to the way Amy had been surprisingly willing to go to bed the night the jade tiger disappeared from the gallery. "Amy, did Jimmy have something to do with the theft of the jade tiger?"

Amy began rifling through her closet, finally pulling out a denim jacket. "I can't tell you any more now," she said. She slipped on the jacket. "My dad's waiting for me downstairs."

Nancy, George, and Bess sat on the beach at Cherry Creek, watching the waves wash up against the shore. It was still early in the day, and fog hung over the water, enclosing the beach in soft, sleepy mist.

"I'm zonked," Bess said, flopping down on the blanket with a yawn.

116

"Me, too," admitted the usually energetic George. "This kidnapping business can really wear you out." She squinted up at Nancy, who still sat staring out to sea. "What do you think is going on at the police station?"

Nancy shrugged. "I'm not sure. I know Terry's going to show Detective Brower the note. Except for the signature, it was printed in block letters. I don't know if the police will be able to trace that."

"So you're back on the case," George concluded.

Nancy smiled. "I talked to Amy this morning. It turns out the mysterious Jimmy Thieu is a friend of hers. But he's also Mr. Mai's nephew, and he knows what goes on in the gallery. I'd bet anything he knows who stole the trunk and what was in it. He may even know who stole the jade tiger from the gallery."

George frowned. "Didn't he sic a Doberman on you?"

"Not exactly," Nancy said. "He just didn't stop it the second time."

"He still doesn't sound too friendly," Bess said in a worried voice. "How are you going to get him to talk to you?"

"Good question," Nancy said. "And how am I going to find him without alerting his uncle?"

"Doesn't he live with his uncle above the gallery?" George asked. "We could wait for him outside."

"*We* are going to a wedding rehearsal," Bess reminded her cousin.

George shut her eyes. "Joanne added me to the wedding procession. Bess is supposed to carry wildflowers, and I'm supposed to carry a set of gongs or something."

"Bells," Bess corrected her. "You're carrying a set of Japanese bells."

Nancy grinned. "Thanks for the answer to my question. I'll wait for Jimmy near the gallery and pray I don't run into Mr. Mai."

Shortly after Keith picked up Bess and George for the wedding rehearsal, Nancy parked her car a few blocks from the Fe T'sui Gallery. She looked at her watch. It was almost three. She had no idea where Jimmy Thieu might be on a Saturday afternoon. She hoped he was somewhere nearby. What she needed was a spot from which she could safely observe the gallery.

A sidewalk café diagonally across from the gallery seemed to be the perfect place—*if* Mr. Mai didn't spot her first. Nancy sat down at one of the outdoor tables and ordered an iced tea. Then she opened a newspaper in front of her face and began the waiting game. The air had gotten cooler, she noticed, and the fog hadn't lifted. She peered over the top of the paper. The fog completely covered the bay.

Nancy didn't have long to wait. About fifteen minutes after she sat down, she saw Jimmy's slight figure in the distance, walking up from the bay. Nancy paid for her tea and made her way down the hill, careful to keep to the side of the street. She didn't want Jimmy to see her until the last minute. She was sure he would run if he did.

She was about forty yards away from the boy when he spotted her. He immediately turned back toward the water.

118

"Jimmy, please wait!" Nancy called out. "I need to talk to you."

He ignored her.

"Amy was kidnapped!" Nancy shouted at his back.

The boy stopped and slowly turned to face her. "What?"

"She was kidnapped by a man who drives a dark red car," Nancy said, walking slowly toward the boy. "She's home now and all right, but if you know who he is, I need your help."

Jimmy's dark eyes were unreadable. At last he said, "This isn't a good place to talk. Meet me in an hour by the cove in Tennessee Valley."

Nancy remembered passing the sign for the beach earlier that week. "All right," she said, hoping she could trust him. "One hour."

Tennessee Valley, Nancy mused as she pulled into the parking lot for the beach. What an odd name for a place in northern California. A sign at the head of the trail explained that the valley was named after a ship, the *Tennessee,* that had gone down just offshore in 1853. Nancy shivered as she read the description. The day was rapidly getting cooler, and the fog seemed even thicker than before.

Nancy pulled her jacket tightly around her and set off down the trail that led to the beach. A rider on horseback passed her, the muffled sound of the horse's hooves making her aware of just how quiet it was. It's a good thing I arrived early, Nancy thought to herself. This trail must be well over a mile long. She wondered if Jimmy was already waiting for her.

119

The trail wound downhill to the ocean. Nancy noticed that as she got closer to the water, the fog thickened. By the time she reached the small cove, she could barely see ten feet in front of her. This feels too much like the first time I met Jimmy, she thought, remembering the chase through the redwoods.

And then a shadow slipped out from behind the rocks at the edge of the beach, and Jimmy Thieu was standing before her. "What happened to Amy?" he asked at once.

Nancy told him, finishing with a question of her own. "Do you know the man in the dark red car?"

The boy shrugged. "I know he's the one who broke into Amy's house and stole the trunk," he answered matter-of-factly.

"Because the jade tiger was hidden inside it?"

"I'm not sure," Jimmy said. "All I know is he brought the trunk to my uncle. He must have sold it to him."

"What else can you tell me?" Nancy asked.

Jimmy picked up a stone and threw it into the water. The beach was now so fogged in that Nancy couldn't even see the ocean.

"He's big and blond," Jimmy said. "Over six feet tall. His name is Malcolm Elgar, and the first time he got in touch with my uncle, he called from Thailand. I know because I took the phone call."

This was more information than Nancy had expected to get from the boy.

Jimmy's next words took her by surprise. "Is he after you?"

"It sounds that way," Nancy said truthfully. "I

think he kidnapped Amy as a warning to me to drop the case."

"Then you're crazy if you don't drop it," Jimmy said. "I don't know much about Elgar except that he's dangerous. You only have to be around him about two seconds to pick up on that." He shook his head angrily, and the silver earring glimmered in the dull light. "If you care about Amy, then don't mess with Malcolm Elgar."

"If you care about Amy, why didn't you tell her any of this?" Nancy asked. "Why didn't you warn her?"

The boy's eyes flashed with anger. "I tried. That's why I went up there the night of the storm. But she wasn't home. And every time I tried to call, her father answered the phone."

Nancy sighed with exasperation. "You couldn't have forced yourself to talk to Terry?"

"No," Jimmy said.

"Why—" But before she could finish her sentence, the boy ran off into the fog. "Jimmy!" she called. "Jimmy! Wait!"

There was no answer. He was gone. Great, Nancy thought as a light drizzle began to fall. It's going to be a lot of fun trying to find the car in this. She wished she'd brought a flashlight.

It seemed forever before Nancy found her way back through the dense fog. With a sense of relief, she got into the car and flipped on the switch for the lights. The lights didn't go on. Feeling a little uneasy, Nancy turned the key in the ignition. There was no response. She tried again, but the car wouldn't start. Perfect,

Nancy thought grimly, the battery's dead. Now I have to walk around in this fog until I can find a phone and get someone to recharge the battery.

Sighing, she reached for the door handle, only to hear a click. Her door had just been locked—by someone who was in the back seat.

14

An Odd Reunion

Nancy tensed when she heard the click. Who was in the back seat—Jimmy? She was sure he hadn't come up from the beach with her. She was afraid of whom she might see if she turned around to look.

"Just keep quiet and you won't get hurt," said a man's voice. "Do you think you can do that?"

Nancy nodded. What good would screaming do? The sound would never carry from inside the car.

"I believe you've been looking for me," the man said.

"You're Malcolm Elgar, aren't you?"

"Try Nick Finney."

Slowly Nancy turned to face him.

Nicholas Finney looked nothing like the fair-haired man who drove the dark red car. He looked exactly as Terry had described him: a slight, wiry man with bright red hair and small, pointed features. His face looked surprisingly young. If it weren't for the fine lines around his eyes and mouth, Nancy would have thought he was in his early twenties.

They stared at each other for a moment. "What did you do to the car?" Nancy asked as calmly as she could.

"Disconnected some wires. I'll hook them up again," he offered casually, "if you'll set up a meeting for me with Terry Kirkland."

"You didn't need me for that," Nancy said. "Terry still thinks of you as a friend. He'd have been glad to see you."

A flicker of something that might have been surprise crossed Nick's face. "Then there's no problem, is there? You can just take me to him."

Nancy found that her fear was quickly being replaced by anger. "Did you follow Terry to the show, destroy his work, and leave your dog tags as a greeting card? Why should I believe you're Terry's friend? How do I know that you're not going to kill him?"

Nick lowered his eyes. "I'm not going to kill anyone," he said softly. "And I'm not the one who wrecked his show. I haven't seen my dog tags since the day I was taken prisoner of war. They were stolen from me."

Nancy still wasn't satisfied. "If you wanted to see Terry, why didn't you just call him?" she asked. "You didn't need to scare me half to death."

"I didn't think he'd want to see me," Nick said quietly. "Not after all that's happened—the break-ins, his daughter being kidnapped and all."

"Which you weren't responsible for?"

Nick gave her an angry, indignant look. "Terry was my *friend*."

124

"Then how do you know about all those things?" she asked suspiciously.

Nick's expression hardened. "I'll explain everything to Terry. Now I want you to find a phone and tell him I need to see him. I'll reconnect your wires."

Nancy looked out at the wall of fog surrounding the car. "Where am I going to find a phone in this weather?"

Nick reached into his pocket and produced a flashlight. Then he gave her directions to the nearest pay phone, which he said was within walking distance. "Tell Terry to meet me at Ross," he said. "He'll know what I mean."

Nancy set off into the thick fog, wondering if she'd lost her mind. She was helping Nick Finney, who might or might not be extremely dangerous. Worse, she was about to draw Terry into this, too. Maybe she should call the police instead. Maybe she should just vanish into the fog and let Nick find Terry on his own. Why don't I? she wondered. The answer came to her at once: Nick Finney was trusting her. And in a weird way it made her feel that she had to trust him.

Nancy made the phone call to Terry and returned to the car to find the engine running and Nick Finney sitting in the driver's seat. "Get in," he said.

She got in next to him, feeling suddenly uneasy. What if Nicholas Finney had been lying all along? What if he wasn't going to meet Terry? What if he had other plans for her? She just had to hope that he'd told the truth, or that she'd be able to find a way out of the situation.

"What did Terry say?" Nick asked abruptly.

"That he'd meet you at the entrance to Fort Ross,"

Nancy reported truthfully. "He'll be there in about an hour. He's taking Amy to a friend's house first."

"That's a good idea," Nick said, pulling out of the Tennessee Valley parking lot.

"Fort Ross is up by the Russian River, isn't it?" Nancy asked, wanting to keep him talking.

"Yes. I grew up near there, by the fort."

"There's a lot of history on the coast," Nancy said. "And a lot between you and Terry," she added. "Malcolm Elgar is part of it, too, isn't he?"

Nick slid her a sharp, appraising look. "Very good," he said in a light tone. "But I'm not answering questions now."

Nick kept his word. Although Nancy repeatedly tried to draw him into conversation, he ignored her questions.

They rode north along the coast, past Mount Tamalpais, past the wide open waterway where the Russian River flowed into the Pacific. As they traveled north, the fog lifted. By the time they reached the fort's redwood stockade, a clear blue dusk had fallen.

Terry's van was parked at the entrance to the fort. Nancy could see him standing on the driver's side. Nick pulled up alongside him and rolled down the window. "Follow me," he said. Before Terry could respond, Nick pulled away, heading for the winding road above the sea. The tires squealed as he took a curve at a good fifteen miles above the speed limit.

"Would you please slow down," Nancy said, holding on to the door handle. "What are you doing?"

"Making sure we're not being followed by anyone except Terry," Nick answered.

For the next ten minutes he led Terry on a mad ride

above the cliffs, swerving fast and tight. More than once Nancy shut her eyes, sure that they'd never make the curve and the car would be sent flying into the ocean.

At last Nick veered off the highway and onto a narrow road. Nancy looked behind them and was relieved to see that Terry had survived the roller coaster ride.

Nancy felt her tense muscles relax as Nick turned onto a dirt road and stopped the car beneath a stand of redwoods. Terry pulled up beside them a few minutes later. He and Nick got out of their vehicles at the same moment. By the light of their headlights, the two men who hadn't seen each other since they were teenagers stood absolutely still. Each looked as if he couldn't believe what he saw.

"Kirkland," Nick said softly.

Terry's voice was hoarse with amazement. "I thought you were dead all these years."

Nick shook his head. "I was almost dead. More than once." He gave Terry a reckless grin. "Don't understand it myself, but the Pilot still hasn't caught up with me."

"I'm glad," Terry said.

Fascinated, Nancy watched the reunion. Both Terry and Nick looked as if they thought the other might disappear at any second, as if the entire night might be a dream.

"I'm not the one who kidnapped your daughter," Nick said abruptly.

"I know," Terry told him. "I never thought you were."

"But I know who did." Nick looked at Nancy for

127

the first time since they'd gotten out of the car. "And so does she. Let's find a place to talk."

Nick led the way up a wooded slope on the side of the road. Nancy walked behind the two men. Night had fallen. She could barely see Nick ahead of her, and she couldn't hear either man. Both of them wove through the dark woods silently. What a day, she thought wryly. First the fog and now a pitch-black forest. I wouldn't be surprised if quicksand were next.

Terry startled her from her thoughts by suddenly appearing at her side. "This way," he said, nodding toward a small clearing to the left.

Nick sat on a large boulder that appeared white in the moonlight. "Sorry," he said to Nancy as she entered the clearing. "I know all this hide-and-seek stuff seems extreme, but if I'm right, there's a good chance we're being followed by Elgar."

"Malcolm Elgar?" Terry echoed. "The guy who thought he was a ninja?"

"You've got it," Nick said grimly. "Elgar was trained for intelligence work," he explained to Nancy. "That means that while he was in the military, he learned a lot about how to get in and out of places without being seen. And how to do a lot of damage. From what I can tell, he picked up a few nasty tricks on his own after that." His eyes met Terry's. "He's deadly."

"He didn't kill Amy," Terry pointed out.

"That's only because he was using her as a warning. You might not be so lucky next time."

"Why is Elgar following you?" Nancy asked.

Nick ran a hand through his red hair. "I guess you

could say we're following each other. I'm beginning to feel like I've been following him since the day our unit was hit."

"You mean the day you were declared missing in action?" Nancy asked.

Nick nodded. "What actually happened was that all of us who weren't killed were taken captive. I spent the next three years in a prison camp." His voice tightened as he continued. "I'm not going to go into what went on there. Let's just say that three years later I was very happy to escape."

"And then what?" Terry asked. "Where have you been since then?"

"Thailand mostly," Nick replied. "Somehow, after being a POW, coming back to the States just didn't make sense to me."

"Then why did you come back now?" Nancy wanted to know.

"Malcolm Elgar." Nick picked up a stick from the ground and snapped it angrily in two. "I ran into him a few months ago in Bangkok. I couldn't believe it. I was sure he'd been killed in that attack, since he certainly wasn't taken prisoner. We had this big, emotional reunion. And while we were talking, he started telling me that he was looking to buy Burmese jade, the real light translucent stone. He said it was worth a fortune. Which reminded me of something I hadn't thought about in years."

"The jade tiger," Nancy and Terry said at once.

"Right. I made the mistake of telling Elgar about it. I said, 'I used to have a statue made of that stuff. I didn't know it was all that valuable. Found it in a Vietnamese temple we looted.'"

Nancy wanted to make sure she understood this. "You stole the jade tiger from a temple?"

Nick shrugged and looked slightly embarrassed. "The temple was deserted. There weren't any monks there or anything. Not that it excuses doing it, but a lot of guys in our unit were helping themselves. These things happen in war.

"Anyway," Nick went on, "I told Elgar I'd found a jade tiger like that years ago, and I'd given it to you, Terry, to hold for me."

"Why did you tell him that?" Nancy asked.

"I guess I was all caught up in the excitement of seeing an old buddy I'd thought was dead. It didn't occur to me that Elgar wasn't a friend until the day after we met. That's when something he said hit me funny."

"He was showing interest in the jade tiger?" Terry guessed.

"No," Nick answered. "We were talking about that last mission. And Elgar said, 'I knew that hill was trouble from the start. I never liked those coordinates.'"

Nick's answer didn't sound terribly sinister to Nancy, and her face must have shown it. Nick was quick to explain. "The coordinates are the numbers on a map that tell you exactly where a mission will take place."

"And this mission was top secret," Terry said, following Nick's train of thought. "Which means that Elgar shouldn't have had those coordinates."

"Exactly," Nick said. "The only ones who should have known our destination were our lieutenant and our sergeant. Both of whom were killed."

"Elgar knew where you were going, and he shouldn't have," Nancy said.

"And the enemy knew where we were going and shouldn't have," Nick said. "That's why we all wound up either dead or prisoners. All except Elgar."

"You think Elgar betrayed your unit," Nancy said, understanding the full meaning of Nick's story.

"He sold our location to the enemy," Nick said. "I spent three years as a prisoner of war because of Malcolm Elgar. And I was one of the lucky ones."

"Have you told anyone else about this?" Nancy asked.

Nick shook his head. "I have no proof. The day I figured this out, I tried to find Elgar in Bangkok and found he'd taken a plane to San Francisco. I knew where he was heading—and what he was after." He looked guiltily at Terry. "I'm sorry. I never should have mentioned your name."

Terry gave his friend a weary grin. "You'd have saved me a lot of trouble if you hadn't. You could have at least warned me that Elgar was in the neighborhood."

"I didn't get back to the States until after he stole the trunk," Nick said. "And even though I've been following him, I swear I didn't know he was going to take your daughter. I would have stopped him."

Nancy barely heard this exchange. She was trying to put together the pieces of the mystery. "Let's say Elgar broke into your house. On the third try he got the tiger," she said to Terry. "Then he sold it to Mr. Mai. So who stole it from Mai?"

Both Nancy and Terry looked at Nick for an answer. But the answer never came. Instead, there was a long, hissing sound in the air and a bright flash overhead.

Terry grabbed Nancy's arm and shouted, "Run! The woods are going to burn!"

15

Fire on the Mountain

Nancy heard a soft thud and then a crackling sound. A bright light blazed above them on the mountain. Birds screamed in alarm, and flames sprang up and swept across the dry forest floor. Nancy watched in horror as the fire began to spread.

"Run!" Nick shouted.

Terry was still beside her. Together they raced downhill toward the road. Nancy pulled back just before they reached the bottom. "Wait," she said to Terry. "Where's Nick?"

They turned and looked up the hill behind them. Silhouetted by orange flames, Nick Finney was crouched on the ground, his arms wrapped around one knee. "He's hurt," Nancy said.

Terry muttered something under his breath and set off back up the hill. Nancy followed at once.

"No!" Terry shouted to Nancy over the roar of the flames. "Go back to the car. Get help!"

"I'm not leaving you here!" Nancy shouted back. It was a long way down. She knew that Terry would need help with Nick if either of them were to make it off the mountain alive.

The flames grew higher as Nancy and Terry drew closer to Nick. Dense black smoke surrounded them. Coughing, Nancy pulled off her jacket and used it to cover her nose and mouth.

Terry was beside Nick now. "My knee went out," Nick gasped. "I can't walk. Get out of here. Just save yourselves."

"Not without you," Terry replied. He grasped Nick under one arm and then looked up at Nancy. "Can you get his other arm?" he asked.

She nodded, and together they managed to pull Nick up. With one arm over Terry's shoulders and one over Nancy's, Nick balanced between them. Leaning heavily on Terry, he slowly began to hobble down the mountain.

Nancy felt the heat of the flames at her back. The fire seemed to be racing down the mountain. The smoke was so dense she could barely see ahead of her. She and Terry and Nick moved slowly, stumbling into rocks and trees. All of them were choking. How much longer do we have? Nancy wondered. She fought down a wave of fear, forcing herself not to look back at the blaze behind them. Just keep moving, she told herself.

Then, above the roar of the fire, Nancy heard a welcome sound: sirens. Seconds later she saw flashing lights below them.

Nancy didn't know whether they would have made it off the mountain if the fire department hadn't arrived when they did. A burly fireman grabbed Nick and carried him down. Two others helped Nancy and Terry. Then they went to work trying to bring the fire under control.

Nearly three hours later Nancy and Terry left the local hospital. Nick was staying overnight, since the doctors wanted to x-ray and treat his knee. She and Terry had been treated for smoke inhalation and pronounced well enough to go home.

Nancy and Terry stood in the hospital parking lot, their clothes and faces still black from the smoke.

"Terry," Nancy said, "what started the fire?"

"Someone shot a signal flare onto the mountain," he replied. "Because of the drought, the mountainside is like tinder. The second the flame hit the ground, it caught fire. It will probably take the fire department all night to put it out."

"Do you think Malcolm Elgar started it?"

"That's my guess," Terry said, getting into his van. "That's what Nick and I told the fire department."

Nancy thought about her adventures with Detective Brower. "We're lucky they didn't hold *us* as suspects."

"Well, I'm sure there'll be an investigation, but for tonight they were willing to believe us."

"Nancy, wake up!"

Nancy opened one eye to find Bess leaning over her. She opened her other eye and realized that Bess had bright pink curlers in her hair.

"Joanne's getting married today," Bess informed her. "George and I let you sleep late because of the fire last night, but you've really got to start getting ready."

Reluctantly Nancy sat up in bed. The day before had left her exhausted. She'd nearly forgotten about Joanne's wedding in all the excitement.

"Breakfast is served," George announced, coming into the bedroom with juice and muffins on a tray.

"Do you want me to give you a manicure?" Bess asked.

Nancy examined her fingernails and grinned. "No, thanks. I'm just glad all the black washed off. It's nice to see them clean again."

"So," George said, settling down beside her, "the mystery is solved."

"Part of it," Nancy agreed with a yawn. "We know that Elgar was the one who broke into Terry's house and the one who kidnapped Amy. And Jimmy Thieu is pretty sure Elgar sold the tiger to his uncle. But we don't know who stole the tiger from the gallery."

"What about Nick Finney's dog tags showing up in the middle of Terry's art show?" Bess asked.

"Nick told Terry that his dog tags were stolen the day he was taken prisoner of war. Elgar must have had them all this time."

"So now what?" George asked.

"The police have all the information we do, and after the kidnapping and arson, they're really after Elgar. Let's hope they get him, because"—she stood up, went to the closet, and took out a pale blue dress—"I'm going to a wedding!"

Nancy walked through the double doors of the huge barn and laughed with delight. She'd known all

136

along that Joanne would have a memorable wedding, but what she saw was even more amazing than she'd expected. Garlands of fresh flowers were draped from the rafters. Japanese silk fans hung on the rough wooden walls. There were ribbons and bells, bows and balloons everywhere. A band was set up in one of the lofts above, playing a mix of rock, country, and jazz. Tables heaped with food lined the huge room. Although it was still early, the barn was already crowded with guests.

Beside her, Amy tugged on her hand. "Hi," Nancy said. She looked around the room, not seeing Terry. "Where's your dad?"

Amy smiled. "He met some artist he knows, and they're talking galleries. What I want to know is, where's the famous wedding cake?"

"Good question," Nancy said. "Let's go find it." She and Amy made their way to the opposite end of the barn, where an entire table had been given to the cake. Nancy couldn't quite believe it, but Joanne had turned the sheets of chocolate-carrot cake into a beautiful fairy-tale castle, frosted in pink and white.

"It's awesome," Amy said.

"It sure is," Nancy agreed with a grin.

"Where are Bess and George?" Amy asked.

"I guess they're with the others getting ready for the wedding march. Come on." Nancy nodded toward the rows of folding chairs. "Let's find good seats."

But by the time Nancy had threaded her way through the crowd to the seats she wanted, Amy was no longer at her side. She turned and scanned the room, looking for the girl.

"Have you seen Amy?" Terry asked, coming up beside her.

"She was right here a minute ago," Nancy said.

Terry's eyes held a familiar dread. "Not again," he said softly.

"Why don't you take this end of the room, and I'll take the other?" Nancy said quickly. "If we don't see her, we'll call the police."

Terry agreed, and they began searching the crowded barn. This is ridiculous, Nancy thought. The wedding procession was due to start in half an hour, and the barn was becoming more crowded by the minute. It seemed as if Joanne had invited all of northern California to her wedding. Nancy caught her breath when she saw a young girl with straight black hair, but her heart sank when she saw it wasn't Amy. After checking the musician's loft, Nancy met Terry at the door of the barn. "No luck?" he asked.

She shook her head.

"I'm going to take the van and find the nearest phone to call the police," he said.

"I'll keep looking," Nancy promised. Maybe Amy went outside, she thought, though she couldn't imagine why. Still, it couldn't hurt to take a look around the barn.

Nancy circled the barn and then the silo, which was a short distance away. There was no sign of Amy anywhere. Just as her friends had described it, the farm sat on a bluff overlooking the Pacific. Acres of open green land spread down toward the ocean. Nancy began walking toward the water.

She hadn't gotten far when she noticed a stand of

oak trees. They were old trees, their branches nearly touching the ground. Nancy nearly passed by them before she realized that the low branches would provide a perfect cover. They were one of the few places on the farm where someone might be concealed.

Cautiously she approached the trees and heard the sound of voices. They were definitely young voices, Nancy decided. Her fear gone, she walked into the stand of oak trees and found Jimmy Thieu handing Amy Kirkland a brown paper bag.

"What's going on here?" Nancy demanded.

Both kids looked at her guiltily, but neither answered.

"How could you disappear like that?" she asked Amy. "Don't you know your father's worried sick? He's calling the police right now."

"Oh, great," Jimmy muttered.

"And what are you doing here?" Nancy asked him. "Don't tell me Joanne invited you to the wedding, too."

Jimmy stared at a knothole on the tree, refusing to meet her eyes.

"Amy," Nancy said more gently, "please tell me what's going on. To begin with, what's in the bag?"

Amy looked as if she might answer, but Jimmy said something to her in Vietnamese, and she clutched the bag to her chest.

"I'll tell you what's in the bag, Miss Drew," said a strange voice behind Nancy. "It's what you've been searching for all along."

Nancy turned to look at who was behind her, but

she wasn't fast enough. A gloved hand clamped over her mouth, and another hand held a knife to her neck.

"Amy is holding the jade tiger," the voice continued. "And she's going to give it to me right now. Because if she doesn't, that'll be the end of Nancy Drew."

16

Case Closed

Nancy winced as the jagged blade pressed against her throat. She had no doubt in her mind who held the knife. She had finally found Malcolm Elgar. And once again he had found the jade tiger.

"Amy, he means it," Jimmy said quickly. "Give him the bag!"

Nancy watched Amy's eyes widen with terror. The girl didn't move, and Nancy knew why. She recognized the man who had kidnapped her, and she was paralyzed with fright.

"No?" asked the menacing voice behind Nancy. "You won't give it to me?"

"Amy," Jimmy said sharply, "give it to him now!"

Numbly Amy held out the paper bag. A black-gloved hand reached out and took it.

But Elgar didn't let go of Nancy. "I'll tell you what's going to happen next," he said. "You two kids are going to go back to the wedding. You're going to have a good time. You aren't going to say a word to anyone about what's happened here. In fact, you're both going to forget you ever saw me."

"No," Amy said, her courage returning. "I'm not going to pretend for you."

"You will," Elgar insisted, "because I'm taking Miss Drew here with me, as a sort of insurance policy. If you tell anyone what happened, or if I even suspect that the police are on my trail, she dies. Do you understand?" When neither Jimmy nor Amy answered, Elgar lifted the blade so that it hovered just above Nancy's skin. "You may speak, Miss Drew," he said. "Tell them to forget they ever saw me."

"D-do as he says," Nancy said, pretending to stammer with fear. And then she drove her heel down hard onto Malcolm Elgar's instep.

Elgar cried out in pain as Nancy broke from his grip. "Run!" she shouted to Jimmy and Amy.

Jimmy shouted something in Vietnamese, and he and Amy took off in opposite directions. Good, Nancy thought as she ran, they're scattering. That will make it harder for Elgar. But though Jimmy and Amy were out of reach, Nancy was not as lucky. The high heels and dress she'd worn for the wedding made running nearly impossible. Frantically she kicked off the heels. It helped, but she was still slowed by having to run in stocking feet.

Fortunately Elgar was limping on the foot she had stomped. But when Nancy glanced over her shoulder, she saw that he was gaining on her.

She stumbled suddenly and fell to her knees.

Elgar advanced on her, the knife upraised. "You shouldn't have done that," he said.

142

Nancy felt fear rise in her throat as she got to her feet. She didn't dare turn her back on him now. He was too close. Slowly she backed away from him, moving toward the barn.

"Not that way," Elgar said. "Toward the ocean. I think, Ms. Drew, you're going to have an accidental fall from the cliff."

Nancy slowly circled, keeping her eyes on Elgar. "Terry's already called the police," she told him. "You'll be facing charges for arson, theft, and kidnapping. Do you really want to add murder to the list?"

Elgar's eyes narrowed and then widened as he stared at something behind Nancy.

"Murder's been on his list for a long time now," Nick Finney said.

Nancy felt Nick's hand on her arm, gently pulling her out of the way. She saw that he had a gun trained on Elgar. "Go back to the wedding," he told her. "This is between Elgar and me."

"Nick, what are you going to do?" Nancy asked uneasily.

"Nothing, as long as my old buddy here doesn't give me any trouble."

"I won't give up," Elgar said calmly. "You're going to have to kill me." He pointed to Nick's pants leg, which was swollen at the knee with bandages. "Do you really think you can take me?" he taunted.

Nancy heard footsteps behind her, turned, and felt herself relax for the first time since Amy had vanished from the wedding. Terry Kirkland was running toward them, with three police officers close behind.

* * *

Nancy helped herself to a chunk of wedding cake. "Delicious," she said to Joanne.

"Thanks to all of you," Joanne said to Nancy, Bess, and George.

"Did you like the ceremony?" Keith asked.

Nancy smiled at her friends. "It was definitely the most unusual wedding I've ever seen." She looked at Joanne's white silk kimono. "And your wedding gown is gorgeous."

Joanne lifted one arm, trailing a long brocade sleeve. "It was everything I dreamed it would be," she said. "Except for that business with Malcolm Elgar. Is that whole mess straightened out now?"

"We'll find out," Nancy said. "The police arrested Elgar—and Nick, too, because he had a gun. When Terry found out that Jimmy was trying to give Amy the jade tiger, he insisted on taking them both home to find out what their story was."

"Who has the tiger now?" Bess asked.

"The police," Nancy replied. "We'll get our answers soon enough. But for now, I think it's time we had some fun!"

"Let's hit the dance floor," Bess said as the band started up.

"It was great of Terry to ask us to stay an extra week," Bess said the next day as the three friends returned from the beach.

"He said he wanted us to enjoy Cherry Creek under normal conditions," Nancy explained. "Without a mystery driving us all crazy."

"What he doesn't know," George said, "is that Nancy isn't really happy without a mystery."

144

Nancy laughed. "I won't mind this week at all—hiking, swimming, bicycle riding." She grinned at Bess. "We can even take mud baths. But there are still a few loose ends to be tied up."

As the girls approached the house, they saw a white car parked outside. "Maybe," Nancy continued, "they're about to be tied up right now."

Inside the house they found Terry and Nick in the living room.

"Have a seat," Terry said to the three girls. "I'm just about to serve lemonade and cookies. We're going to celebrate."

"What are we celebrating?" Bess asked.

"The police have dropped all charges against me," Nick reported happily. "And they've got Elgar for everything we thought he was guilty of, plus gunrunning. That's how he supported himself after the war. He sold illegal U.S. weapons in Southeast Asia."

"A lovely man," George said.

"And," Nick went on, "once I got back to northern California, I realized I'd missed it here. So I'm going to stay. I'm looking for a place to rent."

"Where have you been staying all this time?" Bess asked curiously.

"In a motel," Nick replied, grinning.

"What about Elgar?" George asked.

"Elgar was camping out," Terry replied. "In the woods on my property."

"That's really creepy," Nancy said. "He was the one who was watching me during the stakeout."

"Then why didn't any of us see him?" George asked.

"Malcolm Elgar hid in the jungles of Vietnam for

145

years and managed to avoid the entire U.S. military," Nick reminded her. "After that, concealing himself in a nice, safe redwood forest really wasn't a problem."

Bess helped herself to a cookie. "What I don't get," she said, "is why he kept bothering Terry after he stole the trunk and sold the tiger to Mr. Mai."

"I'm not sure about this," Nick admitted, "but I think he knew I'd come after him, and that I'd come straight to Terry's. So he waited. And while he waited he realized that Nancy was on his trail." Nick nodded toward Nancy. "He did everything he could to scare you off. And when that didn't work he decided to scare Terry."

Nancy shuddered. "I'm just glad he's the one in jail. For a while there I thought it might be me. I was so relieved when Detective Brower called to say he'd no longer need me for questioning. I called Alison Sayers to let her know."

"None of this explains who took the jade tiger from the gallery," George said.

"That story," Terry said, standing up, "will have to wait for this evening when Amy's home from school."

Nancy had just finished setting the table when she heard the unmistakable sound of a dirt bike. She looked out the window. "Jimmy's here," she said to Amy, who was filling a vase with flowers.

Amy smiled. "I know. My dad invited him."

"I thought Jimmy didn't trust grown-ups," Nancy said.

"He doesn't," replied Terry, who was bringing a salad to the table. "But yesterday shook him up. I think he wants to set things right."

Jimmy knocked on the door, and Terry let him in. Jimmy said hello and looked anxiously up at Terry.

"It's all right," Terry told him. "Just make yourself comfortable and enjoy your dinner. We can straighten out this mess afterward."

Nick showed up a few minutes later, and they all enjoyed dinner. Bit by bit Jimmy seemed to relax. Afterward, Terry built a fire, and they all gathered around it.

Terry nodded at his daughter. "I think everyone here wants to know how the jade tiger wound up at the wedding yesterday. Amy, why don't you start?"

Amy took a deep breath. "You know that Malcolm Elgar stole the trunk, and the tiger was hidden in it. Well, Jimmy pretty much guessed that Elgar stole the statue."

"How?" Bess asked.

Jimmy shrugged. "I've been around that gallery for a while now. I know what real collectors look like and sound like. Malcolm Elgar sounded like he had something hot that he had to get rid of. When I asked my uncle about Elgar, he just changed the subject. But he admitted that the statue had 'probably' been looted from a temple. Of course, he'd never say that to anyone else. Galleries aren't supposed to deal in stolen goods, but Uncle Mai doesn't always play by the rules."

"Besides," Amy added, "Jimmy knew the trunk had been stolen from us."

Jimmy grinned. "I figured the statue ought to go back where it belonged—to Vietnam."

"*You* stole it from the gallery," Nancy said.

"It wasn't that hard," the boy explained. "I knew how to shut off the gallery's security system."

"I'm sorry I couldn't tell you, Nancy," Amy said quickly. "I knew Jimmy had it, but I promised I'd keep his secret."

"We'll talk about that one later," her father promised. He looked at Jimmy with one eyebrow raised. "Go on."

Jimmy took a deep breath and continued his story. "After my uncle reported the statue stolen, and the police started searching, I knew I couldn't hang on to it. I figured the police would suspect me of taking it. So I called Amy and asked her if she'd hide it for me, just until I could find a temple in Vietnam that we could send it to."

"Unfortunately," Terry broke in, "Jimmy couldn't get through to Amy until the night before the wedding. He was desperate to get rid of the statue, so Amy told him to meet her on the farm. She figured she'd slip away from the wedding, hide the statue in the van, and no one would ever know."

"Except for Malcolm Elgar," Nancy said. "And me and Terry."

Jimmy turned a deep shade of red. "Maybe it wasn't the greatest plan. I never meant for you to be in danger."

"What does your uncle think of all this?" George asked.

"When he found out the police are holding on to the tiger for evidence, he got real nervous. He told the police he had no idea the statue was stolen. He also broke the deal with the person who bid on it. He's even volunteered to donate the price of the statue to an organization for Vietnamese refugees."

"But what about you?" Nancy asked. "I get the feeling you're not too happy living there."

Jimmy shrugged. "I'm not, but the police are watching Uncle Mai right now. He'll do anything to prove he's a good, upright citizen, and that means he's got to treat me right."

"And you've a place you can go if he doesn't," Terry added. "You can always come here."

"Will the tiger ever get back to Vietnam?" Nancy wondered.

"I don't know," Terry said, grinning. "But so far it's traveled from a Vietnamese temple, to this house, to an exclusive gallery, to a wedding. Give it enough time, and I bet that jade tiger makes it back home." Terry gave his daughter a curious look. "So, do you still want to be a detective?" he asked.

Amy thought for a moment. "It's pretty neat," she answered, "but I guess I'll leave the detecting to Nancy."

NANCY DREW® MYSTERY STORIES By Carolyn Keene

THE HARDY BOYS® SERIES By Franklin W. Dixon